# New TOEIC Listening Script

*service*

v. ①.服務
②.檢修.保養

n.服務
公共設施 There is a good bus service into the city.

**PART 1**

1. ( A )  (A) They are servicing a bicycle.
   (B) They are searching a room. 搜查一個房間
   (C) They are washing a car. 洗車
   (D) They are towing a boat. 拖船
   tow 拖

2. ( B )  stock 辦貨.屯貨.供給 → 正在上貨
   (A) The clerk is stocking the shelves.
   (B) The professor is giving a lecture. 教課 give sb. a lecture
   面試候選人(C) The manager is interviewing a candidate. 教訓某人
   檢查病人(D) The doctor is examining a patient. n.病人 adj.能忍耐的
   (診斷)   /Ig`zæmIŋ/ 檢查.診察.測驗 in/on
   examine   The teacher examined
   the students in English

3. ( C )  (A) The fireman is climbing a ladder.
   (B) The teacher is closing a window.
   (C) The server is taking a man's order.
   (D) The mechanic is removing a tire.
   技工

a range of hills 一片丘陵

4. ( A )  在等乘客
   (A) The taxis are waiting for passengers.
   (B) The buses are leaving the highway. 公路
   (C) The trucks are parked on the hill. 斜坡
   (D) The trains are leaving the station. 小山丘
   火車要離開車站

U0084653

5. ( C )  (A) Some people are attending a concert. 正在參加演唱會
   (B) Some people are watching a movie. 在看電影
   (C) Some people are leaving the train station. 離開車站
   (D) Some people are sitting in a park. 坐在公園

正在看文件

6. ( A )  type
   (A) The woman is reading some documents.
   (B) The woman is typing on a laptop. 在筆電上打字
   (C) The woman is drinking coffee. laptop computer
   (D) The woman is talking on the phone. = notebook

*GO ON TO THE NEXT PAGE.*

## PART 2

7. ( B )  What time does the next train to San Diego leave? 下班往San Diego的火車何時離開?
   (A) At the next stop. 下一站   * therapy   → therapist
   (B) In half an hour. 半小時    [θεrəpɪ]    n.治療醫家
   (C) About 10 dollars. 大約10元    n.治療.療法

8. ( B )  Did you go to the doctor yesterday? 你昨天有去看醫生嗎?
   (A) It's a new type of therapy. 是新式治療法
   (B) Yes, that's why I left work early. 這是為何我提早離開公司
   (C) Some friends from school.

9. ( A )  My car broke down on Fontana Boulevard.
   break down 失效,停止運轉 → Her health broke down under the pressure of work.
   (A) OK, I'll send someone to pick you up.
   (B) It's about 20 miles.
   (C) Some new business cards.
   有新的名片
   工作的壓力把她的身體弄垮了
   └→ 介副詞,亦後無O.

10. ( A )  The sale promotion was a big success, wasn't it? 特價促銷很成功,對吧?
    (A) Yes, it went very well. 進行得很順利
    (B) By the end of the month. 這個月底        * 挪用公款者
    (C) He's at a conference in Los Angeles. 他在LA開會   a deffalcator
                                                              x  e

11. ( C )  這裡的員工每週還是兩週一次收到薪資?
    Do employees here receive weekly or bi-weekly paychecks?
    (A) Only a year-end bonus. 只有年終       an embezzler
    (B) At the bank on the corner. 在轉角的銀行   into destroy
    (C) They get paid every Friday.
    每週五被付錢(領薪)

12. ( C )  Where can I find the vacation request forms? 那裡可以找到休假申請表格
    (A) To Denver and Chicago.
    (B) A revised itinerary. 修正過的行程表   * revise v.修正.校正
    (C) In the file cabinet by the door.   * itinerary  n.旅程.旅行計畫
    門口的文件櫃 ①櫃.內閣               [aɪtɪnə,rɛrɪ]

13. ( A )  Please watch your step as you exit the building → Each member of the cabinet
    離開大樓  (A) Sure, I'll be careful. 恰當      stated his views on the question.
    時注意腳步 (B) At the board meeting. → 董事會   每位內閣成員就這一問題談了自己
              (C) About 45 minutes.                 的想法

14. ( C )  和客戶吃飯的錢如何付?
    How will I pay for dinner with the client?
    (A) Last night at 8 o'clock.  * 公款 public money   government expense
    (B) Business formal.          funds
    (C) Use the company credit card.  上

15. ( A ) Do you want to go to the concert tonight? 你今天想去演唱會嗎?
   (A) What time is the show? 表演何時開始?
   (B) A new guitar. 新吉他
   (C) Charlie found one this morning.

※ decision → worst of all, he /dɪˈsɪʒən/ had no hope of shaking her resolution.
① 決定 ② 決心
最糟的是他無活動搖她的決心

16. ( C ) When is the Thrask deal going to be finalized? settlement
   這個案子何時會結案
   (A) No, that was a good meal. 因那餐很好吃 resolution
   (B) There's a collection bin on the second floor. 二樓有回收桶
   (C) Their CEO's out of the country this week.
   CEO這週不在國內

17. ( A ) How did you hear about our consumer survey?
   知道          客戶調查 (消費者調查)
   (A) I read about it in the newspaper.
   (B) How can I help you? 我該如何幫助你?
   (C) That's where I'm going. 那正是我要去的地方。

You'll hear about this later!
你就等著瞧吧
你一定會被罵!

18. ( A ) We should hire some workers, shouldn't we? 我們該雇用一些人員, 對吧?
   (A) Yes, that's a good idea. 好主意
   (B) Friday afternoon at 3:30.          ※ fill out a form
   (C) Fill out an expense report. 填寫消費報告   ※ Her cheeks have filled out. 兩頰變得豐滿了

19. ( C ) 為何訓練活動重新排程到今天晚一點的時候呢?
   Why was the training session rescheduled for later in the day?
   (A) Thanks. It was a difficult decision. 謝了. 是個困難的決定
   (B) At a location in the city center. 在市中心的某個地點
   (C) You'd have to ask the supervisor.

20. ( B ) 你打算在這裡待多久?          你要問問長官.
   How long are you planning on staying at Coleman Industries?
   (A) For our upstairs neighbor. 給我們樓上鄰居
   (B) I'm not sure of my future plans. 不確定未來的計劃
   (C) We work in the same department. 在同部門工作

21. ( C ) 你對於在餐廳多上一輪班有興趣嗎?
   Are you interested in working an extra shift at the restaurant?
   (A) That customer needs a menu. 客人需要菜單
   (B) Thanks, we already ordered. 謝了. 我們已經訂購了
   (C) Which day would you need me? 你哪天會需要我幫忙?

22. ( A ) 會計部位於哪裡?
   Where is the accounting department located? 位於   located
   (A) Here's the building directory. 樓層介紹   adj. 全都的. 位於的
   (B) Because it wasn't paid. 還沒付錢   well-located buildings
   (C) That seems low. 看起來很低   位置很好的大樓

GO ON TO THE NEXT PAGE.

23. ( B ) Traffic is going to be bad. We should leave soon.
   (A) I left it at home.
   (B) I'll be ready in a few minutes.
   (C) Visit the website.

24. ( B ) Who are we putting on the magazine's <u>front cover</u> this month?
   (A) In the other room.
   (B) We'll decide tomorrow.
   (C) Yes, I wrote the article.

25. ( C ) I think Leah Norkus will get the Employee of the Year award, don't you?
   (A) For dinner on Saturday.
   (B) About a hundred employees.
   (C) Probably. She <u>deserves</u> it.

26. ( B ) On which websites should we <u>publish</u> our advertisements?
   (A) About 500 words.
   (B) Let's try some social media sites.
   (C) I read that already.

27. ( C ) Why hasn't the <u>maintenance</u> crew cleaned up the <u>clothing displays</u>?
   (A) No, the printer is not working.
   (B) Yes, last Tuesday.
   (C) Because they were <u>unloading</u> a truck.

28. ( B ) Aren't you gonna help me do the dishes?
   (A) I've been there before.
   (B) Sorry, I have to make an important phone call.
   (C) The second building on the right.

29. ( C ) Should we <u>inspect</u> the <u>machine shop</u> this morning or this afternoon?
   (A) I got some new T-shirts.
   (B) Please <u>put them in order</u> of time received.
   (C) This afternoon is better for me.

30. ( B ) Who will manage the <u>quality assurance team</u> after Candace leaves?
   (A) In the warehouse district.
   (B) I thought she decided to stay.
   (C) Tickets for the game are sold out.

31. ( A )  The marketing department has a larger budget this quarter. 行銷部門這個季度有比較大的預算.
    (A) Now they can hire more staff. 可以雇多點員工
    (B) He's a junior account executive. 是新的帳戶經理
    (C) Isn't Julie at the technology conference? Julie 不在科技會議上嗎?

＊ 'execute v. 實施, 執行
◎ 處死: to be executed for sth. 因某事被處決

## PART 3

**Questions 32 through 34** refer to the following conversation between three speakers.

M : I beg your pardon, are you the manager? 乞討, 請求  n. 原諒, 寬恕

Woman UK : Yes. Is there a problem, sir? 我點了雞.

M : I ordered the chicken. My server Jenny said it would be out several times, but I'm still waiting. 我的服務生 Jenny 說了好幾次要出餐了. 但我還在等

Woman UK : About how long? 大概多久了呢?

M : At least 25 minutes. 至少 25 分鐘

Woman UK : Oh, that's unreasonable. Let me find out what the holdup is. Jenny, this diner has been waiting nearly half an hour for his meal. 不合理、過份 讓我找出耽擱的原因   用餐者  等待將近半小時

＊ holdup 阻塞. a traffic holdup 補充

Woman US : I'm very sorry. I've asked the chef, but the kitchen is really slow tonight. 我已經問過主廚  餐點  廚房今天晚上很慢(很忙)

Woman UK : I'll ask the chef to send out your meal right away. 我會請主廚馬上將你的餐送出

32. ( D )  Who most likely is the UK woman?
    (A) A travel agent. 旅行社人員
    (B) A bank clerk. 銀行行員
    (C) A warehouse supervisor. 倉庫主管
    (D) A restaurant manager. 餐廳經理

＊ preposterous before / after | adj. /prɪ pɑstərəs/ 十分荒謬的
＊ extravagant /ɪk strævəgənt/ 放肆的 + behaviors + expectations

33. ( A )  What is the man complaining about? 在抱怨什麼?
    (A) An order has not arrived. 訂單沒送到
    (B) A bill is not accurate. 帳單不正確
    (C) An item has been discontinued. 商品沒有生產了
    (D) A reservation was lost. 預約錯過了

＊ excessive /ɪk'sɛsɪv/  outrageous /aut redʒəs/ 過分的
＊ accurate adj. 正確的
＊ reservation ① 預約 ② 異議 ③ 保育區
They accepted the proposal without reservation.

34. ( B )  What does the manager say she will do?
    (A) Delete an account. 刪帳號
    (B) Speak to an employee.
    (C) Refund a purchase. 退款
    (D) Confirm an address. 確認地址

GO ON TO THE NEXT PAGE.

**Questions 35 through 37** *refer to the following conversation.*

我知道你昨天①不用開日被豁行誰開員工會議，所以我想和你說②開會内容

M : Sarah, I know you <u>were excused</u> from the staff meeting we had yesterday, so I wanted to <u>fill</u> 我開另一間牙科診所
<u>you in</u>. I'm planning to open another <u>dental clinic</u>. This one would be in Barrington.

W : Really? Wow! Though... doesn't Barrington seem a little close? It's only a 10-minute drive
from this clinic. Will there be enough business for another location? 前景看好的

從該診所開過去只要10分鐘,那裡會有足夠的生意量嗎? 很有前景的城市(正在進步,發展中的)

M : Yes, I <u>wondered about</u> that <u>initially</u>, but Barrington's an <u>up-and-coming</u> city. Lots of people
are moving there. Plus, we found an <u>unbeatable deal</u> on an <u>available space</u>. I'll go there 我們發現無法超越的交易
tonight so I can view the property again and possibly sign a lease. (超刈算的交易)

我一開始也疑惑

35. ( D ) What are the speakers mainly discussing?
- (A) Hiring a receptionist. 雇權栺人員
- (B) Replacing some <u>outdated</u> equipment. 更換過期設備 可以使用的空間
- (C) Hosting a colleague's <u>retirement party</u>. 主持同事 我今天晚上會再去看看
- (D) Opening another business location. 退休派對 並且可能簽租約
開新的主意點(店)

36. ( A ) What does the man say about the city of Barrington?
- (A) Its <u>population</u> is growing. 人口在增加 ✗ lease
- (B) Its <u>infrastructure</u> is outdated. 基礎建設很過時 n. 租約
- (C) It has a new mayor. 新市長 v. 出租,租得
- (D) It has good <u>public transportation</u>. 好的公眾交通

37. ( C ) What will the man do tonight?
- (A) Attend a dinner. 参加晚宴 ✗ patient adj. 有耐心的
- (B) Film a commercial. 拍廣告 /peʃənt/ n. 病人
- (C) Visit a property. 拜訪.参觀不動産
- (D) Treat a <u>patient</u>. 治療病人 'passion n. 熱情.激情

**Questions 38 through 40** *refer to the following conversation.*

新的啤酒標設計進行得如何了? come along 進展

W : Good afternoon, Steve. How's the new beer bottle label design <u>coming along</u>? Don't forget,
the client wants to see the final design by the end of the week. 客户這周末要看最後的設計

M : The whole team has been working really hard. We've got the basic layout, but we still need
to decide on the color scheme. I'm concerned that we might not be ready for Friday.

整個團隊非常認真,我們有基本的設計但仍需要決定顏色組合,我擔心周五可能不會好

W : Your department always does great work. I'm not <u>terribly concerned</u>. Just please send me
an e-mail on Wednesday letting me know your progress.

M: Thanks. OK, will do. 你的部門總是做的很好, 我並沒有非常擔心

✗ scheme 只要在週三寄email給我知道你的進度就好了
①詭.謀.詭計

That so-called sale is a scheme to swindle the customers.
詐騙

50

38. ( B ) Where do the speakers most likely work? 最有可能在哪裡工作
   (A) At a brewery. 在釀酒廠
   (B) At an advertising agency. 廣告公司
   (C) At an art gallery. 藝廊
   (D) At an amusement park. 遊樂園  ＊ amusement arcade
                                   電子遊樂場  /ar'ked/
                                              n. 拱廊, 騎樓

39. ( C ) What is the man worried about? 擔心什麼
   (A) Hiring qualified employees. 雇用合資格的員工    ＊ qualified
   (B) Correcting a invoice error.                   adj. 合格的
       修正發票錯誤
   (C) Meeting a deadline.                            具備必要條件的
   (D) Responding to customer complaints. 回應客戶的抱怨   勝任的
            v. complain
                                          → She is qualified to do
40. ( A ) What does the woman tell the man to do?          the job.
   (A) Send an update. 寄送更新版本
   (B) Take a day off. 休一天假           We got off immediately after
   (C) Revise an advertisement. 修正,校訂廣告         daybreak.
   (D) Schedule a meeting. 安排會議    黎明後立刻動身
                                              ↗ 下車, 離開 下車

**Questions 41 through 43** refer to the following question between three speakers.

我好意外看到你仍然在辦公室    你通常5:30下班對嗎?
W : Ethan, I'm surprised to see you still at the office. You usually get off at 5:30, right?

Man AUS : Yeah, but I didn't come in until noon today because my car wouldn't start. It's at the
   repair shop getting fixed now. 但我今天一直到中午才進來,因為我的車子發不動.

W : Oh, how are you getting home, then? 在修車店修理中  ＊ not until 直到~才~

Man AUS : I'm waiting for Gerard. He lives in my neighborhood and he offered me a ride home.
   And... Here he comes now. 他住在我附近.他提議載我回家   提供載我一程的好意
        ↷ 驚為頌痛 加油
Man CAN : Hi, Ethan. I'm ready to go, but do you mind if we stop at the gas station on the way
   home? I forgot to fill up this morning on the way to work. 我準備可以走了.但你介意我回家路上

Man AUS : Sure. In fact, let me pay this time. It's the least I can do for all the times you've
   given me a ride. 這次讓我付錢吧            順道經過加油站嗎?
        這動是每次你載我回家我可以        我今天上班路上忘記加油了
41. ( A ) Why is the woman surprised?    做的.
工作很晚 (A) A colleague is working late.
有些文件遺失(B) Some documents are missing.       ＊ all the time
                                               一直向來.一向
成本比預的(C) A cost is higher than expected.
的高  (D) Some projects have been canceled.  →  expect
        有些案子被取消了                        v. 預計.預料.預期

42. ( C ) What problem did Ethan have this morning? 今早遇到什麼問題
    (A) He lost his keys.
    (B) He ordered the wrong item 訂了錯誤的商品
    (C) He had car trouble.
    (D) His mobile phone did not work. 手機壞了

*item 項目,商品,細目
She checked the items in the bill.
檢查了帳單上的帳目

43. ( B ) What does Ethan offer to do? Ethan說可以幫忙什麼?
    (A) Stay late. 待晚一點
    (B) Cover an expense. 負擔開銷
    (C) Check some information. 檢查些資訊
    (D) Submit a receipt. 繳交收據

* offer /'ɔfɚ/
① 給予 He offered me a glass of wine.
② 提議,願意
= He offered to lend me some books.

**Questions 44 through 46** refer to the following conversation.
你因入會來這參加科技研討會對嗎?
W : Leo, you're attending the technology seminar here at the office on Saturday, right? Do you know what time it's supposed to start? 你知道了研討會可能幾點開始嗎?
M : Nine-thirty a.m. It will be led by an outside consultant, Amber Digbee. Oh, and the location has been changed from conference room C to the main conference room.
    九點半! 我很期待這個研討會
W : Oh, good to know. I'm really looking forward to the seminar. I used to work with Amber at my previous job. 我之前的工作有和Amber工作過

44. ( B ) What is the main topic of the conversation? 會由外聘的顧問主持
    (A) A vacation request. 放假請求
    (B) A staff workshop. 員工工作坊
    (C) A client visit. 客戶拜訪
    (D) A marketing campaign. 行銷宣傳活動

lead - led - led
地點從C室換到主要會議室

45. ( C ) According to the man, what recently changed? 根據男生,最近什麼改變了?
    (A) An insurance policy 保險單
    (B) A budget. 預算
    (C) An event location. 活動地點
    (D) A keynote speaker. 主講者
    n.語基調,基本方針

* insurance premium
保險費

The keynote of his speech was that we need peace.
演說重點是需要和平.

46. ( C ) What does the woman say about Amber Digbee?
    (A) She has won an award. 她有得過獎
    (B) She is interviewing for a job. 她在為工作面試
    (C) She used to work with her. 以前和她一起工作
    (D) She read her book. 看了她的書 (沒有"s"一定不是現在式是過去式念/ɛ/)

W : Griffin, are you ready for your relocation to our Singapore offices? 你準備好要搬到我們新加坡辦公室了嗎?

M : It will be my first time living overseas. And I have to find an apartment and learn how things work. 這將會是我第一次住在國外, 我要找一間公寓並學習事情如何運作的

W : Isn't the company helping you get settled? 公司沒有幫忙你安置嗎?

M : Sure, but I mean other than our colleagues, I don't know anyone in Singapore. 有阿, 但我指其他除了我們的同事以外的。我在新加坡不認識任何人

W : Hey, there's a great mobile app you should get called 'Landed'. It will link you to a network of people who just moved to the city. Should be a useful social connection. 有個手機App你一定要有, 叫Landed, 會連結你到剛搬來的人的群。應該是有用的社會聯結

M : Wonderful, I'll check it out. 太棒了, 我會去看

W : Also, I have a travel guide that I used on my last visit to Singapore which has some good information. I'll bring it in for you tomorrow. 我還有本旅遊書上次去新加坡時用的, 裡頭有些好資訊。我明天帶來給你

47. ( D ) What does the man imply when he says, "It will be my first time overseas"?
   (A) He cannot answer a question.
   (B) He is interested in a job offer. 對工作機會有興趣
   (C) He should not be blamed for a mistake. 不應為這錯誤受到責備
   (D) He is nervous about a change.

*blame v. 指責 /e/ 責備

48. ( B ) What does the woman say a mobile app is used for? * mobile adj.
   (A) Personal budgeting. 個人預算劃訂
   (B) Social networking. 社交網路
   (C) Shopping.
   (D) Global positioning. 全球定位 + system (GPS)

/'mobIl/ ✓ 可動的
/'mobɪl/ ✓ 流動的
/'mobaIl/ ✗

49. ( C ) What will the woman give the man? *App = application
   (A) A staff directory. 員工通訊錄
   (B) A business card.
   (C) A book. ⎰ gift
   (D) A voucher. ⎱ luncheon + voucher / phone 禮品卡 午餐券 手機充值卡

* admin = administrative
administrative assistant 行政助理

M : Hey, Sophia, what are you up to? 你在忙什麼? 忙於

W : I'm leading our admin staff meeting today. 我帶領(主持)今天的員工會議 行政

M : Oh, I was expecting Aaron. Is he coming, too? 我以為是Aaron, 他也要來嗎?

W : Aaron has to attend a meeting at district headquarters. 他要參加區總部的會議

M : I see. So what's the meeting about? 明白, 那會議是有關什麼的呢?

GO ON TO THE NEXT PAGE.

W : Mainly about the renovations to the East Annex at the beginning of next month. Since the construction company will be moving floor-by-floor, we'll have to move some classes to different rooms while the work is being done.

*[handwritten annotations: 整修 / n.附加物 / 由於工程公司會一層一層搬，我們要把一些課堂 / v. annex / 移到不同教室，當工程 在進行的時候]*

50. ( A ) Where do the speakers most likely work?
(A) At a school.
(B) At a department store.
(C) At a hotel.
(D) At a factory.

*[handwritten: ①附加= An annex insurance policy was annexed to the contract. / ②併吞= The city annexed the area across the river. / ③得到= She annexed the first prize in the speech contest.]*

51. ( A ) What does the woman mean when she says, "Aaron has to attend a meeting at district headquarters"?
*[handwritten: 同事不能參加會議]*
(A) A co-worker cannot attend a meeting.
(B) A deadline will be extended. *[期限會被延長]*
(C) She is assigning an additional supervisor. *[指派另外的長官]*
(D) She thinks that more staff should be hired.

*[handwritten: 如覺得該雇用更多的員工 / * assign / v.指派、分配 / → Jack was assigned to the assembly shop of the factory. / 被分配到廠裡的 裝配工間]*

52. ( C ) What will happen next month?
(A) A training course will begin. *[開始一個訓練課程]*
(B) Some student interns will arrive. *[有些學生實習生會來]*
(C) Some renovation work will start. *[開始一些整修工作]*
(D) A team will be reorganized.

*[handwritten: 團隊會被重組 / /ˈdʒuəlrɪ/ 珠寶]*

**Questions 53 through 55** refer to the following conversation.

*[handwritten: 這是跳蚤市場的資訊(服務)台嗎？ / 我擁有一間飾品店在市區。]*

W : Hi, is this the information booth for the flea market? I own an accessories shop in town and I'm looking to purchase some beads for my jewelry. *[我想找些珠子搭配我的珠寶]*

M : Oh, welcome to the Swanson Flea Market. If you keep walking straight, you'll see the Hopper's Hobbies booth at the end of this row on the right. They should have beads.

*[handwritten: 在這條走道底端右手邊 / 我從來沒有過這裡，不太確定往哪裡走]*

W : Great. Thank you for your help. I've never been here before and I wasn't sure where to go.

M : Sure, and actually today is the fifth anniversary of this market. There will be a free music festival tonight to celebrate, rain or shine. The first band will start at 6 p.m.

53. ( D ) Where does the conversation take place?
*[handwritten: 當然。而且實際上今天是這個市集的 5週年。今天晚上有免費的慶祝]*
(A) At a library.
(B) At a museum.
(C) At a performing arts center. *[藝術表演中心]* *[音樂節，不論晴雨都會舉辦]*
(D) At an outdoor market. *[戶外市集]*

*[handwritten: 第一個樂團下午6點開始]*

54. ( C ) What does the woman thank the man for? 她為何謝打謝他
   (A) Buying her a ticket. 買票給她
   (B) Approving her registration form. 批准她的註冊表    * approve
   (C) Giving her directions. 給她方向指引         v. 同意. 贊成
   (D) Finding her a seat.                  → The professor does not
       幫她找到椅子                        approve the government's

55. ( B ) What is scheduled for later in the day? 今天晚一點有安排什麼?  foreign
   (A) A lecture. 一堂課                                          policy.
   (B) A concert. 演唱會              * properly
   (C) A beauty contest. 選美比賽     adv. 正確地   properly speaking
   (D) A cooking demonstration.       恰當地    to act properly
       廚藝展示

**Questions 56 through 58** *refer to the following conversation.*

W : Lathrop Music. Can I help you? 我有一間跳舞教室. 有幾個擴聲器無法正常運作
M : Hi, I own a small dance studio and I have a couple of loudspeakers that aren't working
(上)properly. Do you fix sound equipment? 你可以幫我修理嗎?
   我可以修理. 如果你今天拿來(放來店裡)           週五前可以OK
W : Sure, I can repair those. If you drop them off today, they'll be ready by Friday.
                                                        before
M : Actually, I'm flying to a convention in Baltimore on Friday, so I won't be able to pick them up
   then. I can stop by on Monday when I return, though.
我週五去Baltimore參加大會. 我沒有空去取. 我週一回來的時候可以順道去拿.
W : Sounds good. That'll give me more time to work on them. 聽起來不錯. 可以讓我有更多時間
M : Your shop's at 4912 North Beacon Street, right?                    處理
   當你到達的時候, 我建議你停在大樓後
W : That's right, and when you get here, I suggest parking behind the building. There are
   always plenty of spaces available in that area.
       那裡總是有很多位子可以停
56. ( D ) What does the man want the woman to do?
strong (A) Validate a parking stub. →讓停車擋有效(放下㊀.㊁.可以停車)
worth (B) Teach a dance class.              台灣也有人說 搭車地錢
   (C) Listen to some recordings. 聽一些錄音
   (D) Repair some equipment.                    * validate
       修理一些設備                              使有效. 確認. 証實

57. ( C ) Why is the man unavailable on Friday?
   (A) He will be performing. 他要表演         * stub  n. 菸蒂. 殘端
   (B) He has a dentist appointment. 有牙醫預約
   (C) He will be traveling. 會去旅行          * appointment
   (D) He will be visiting a client.          n. 約會. 任命. 委派, 職位
       會去拜訪客戶
                                    I accepted the appointment as
                                    chairman. 同意擔任主席一職

GO ON TO THE NEXT PAGE.

58. ( B )  What does the woman recommend the man do?
   - (A) Find a new instructor. 找新的指導人員
   - (B) Park in a specific location. 在指定地點停車
   - (C) Pay with a credit card. 用信用卡付錢
   - (D) Speak with a manager. 和經理說話

＊住下
tenant   occupant   resident
habitant   dweller   inmate
inhabitant   lodger

同室者. 囚房. 精神病院

**Questions 59 through 61** *refer to the following conversation.*

M : Hi, I'm trying to reach Tiffany Tennant in Personnel.

W : Yes, this is Tiffany.

這是行銷部門來的Ray        有個新員工

M : Hello, this is Ray Biebergal from sales and marketing. A new employee, Jeff Robbins, is starting in my department next week. And I'm wondering how many weeks of vacation new hires receive. 下週開始在我的部門工作. 我在想,新進員工可以有多少週的假期

W : Four weeks a year. That's one of the topics we'll discuss at the new employee orientation. We hold sessions every Monday at 9 o'clock. 那是我們在新訓中會討論到的其中一個話題
我們每週一9:00舉行

M : Thanks for letting me know. I'll make sure Mr. Robbins attends the session. Does he need to sign up in advance? 他需要先登記嗎?

W : Yes, but I can take care of his registration right now. Let's see... Jeff Robbins, yes, I have his new employee file right here. 我現在就可以幫他處理,我看看...有.
我這裡有他的員工檔案

59. ( A )  What department is the man trying to reach? 想聯繫到什麼部門?
   - (A) Personnel. 人事部
   - (B) Information technology. 資訊科技
   - (C) Security. 安管
   - (D) Engineering. 工程

＊orientation
rise
begin

60. ( C )  What does the man inquire about? 詢問
保險索賠 (A) An insurance claim.          into 調查
停車許可證 (B) A parking permit.          after 問候
放假政策 (C) A vacation policy.
   - (D) A weekly expense. 每週開銷

n. ① 培訓 ② 方位, 傾向性
The school has an orientation
towards practical skills.
著重培養實用技能
③ 適應. 熟悉

61. ( B )  What does the woman offer to do?
   - (A) Take a message. 抄留言
   - (B) Register an employee. 幫員工註冊
   - (C) Contact a supervisor. 聯絡長官
   - (D) Reserve a room. 預留房間

W : Hello, I'd like to wire some money to the Philippines.

M : OK, I can help you with that. Have you completed the form?

W : Yes, here it is. Is $15.50 the correct fee?

M : That's right. You're sending less than $1,000.

W : Great. Also, this transfer is somewhat urgent. I'm really hoping it gets there as soon as possible.

M : Well, international transfers can take up to 7 to 10 business days, but they're usually processed much quicker. You can expect it to arrive in a couple of days.

W : That's reassuring. You know, I'm happy your shop has this service. You're right up the block from my house. So, it's really convenient.

M : I'm glad we can help.

62. ( A ) Look at the graphic. What information does the woman have a question about?
    (A) The fee.
    (B) The transaction code.
    (C) The date.
    (D) The recipient.

| Sender | Gwen Finch |
|---|---|
| Recipient | Joaquin Rizal |
| Date | September 22 |
| Amount Sent | $900 US = $46,139 PHP |
| Fee | $15.50 US |
| Transaction Code | DT-01238 |

63. ( D ) What is the woman concerned about?
    (A) Who can sign for a delivery.
    (B) What identification is required.
    (C) Where a package can be picked up.
    (D) When a transfer will arrive.

64. ( B ) What does the woman say about the shop?
    (A) It has a new owner.
    (B) It is close to where she lives.
    (C) It will have a sales event.
    (D) It has been closed recently.

GO ON TO THE NEXT PAGE.

我有間綜合辦公室,我打來詢問你們商圈在賣的木蘭花樹

W : Hello, I manage an office complex and I'm calling about the magnolia trees your nursery

sells.  I think they would make the grounds look very attractive.  I'm looking at your website

now.  我想他們會使土地看起來非常吸引人,我正在看你們網頁  ＊ nursery

M : Sure, do you see our tree size chart?　/n3sərɪ/

有看到我們樹木尺寸表嗎? → 兩種小尺寸差別為何?　n.幼兒室,托兒所.苗圃.漁場

W : Yes, what's the difference between the two smaller types?

M : Type A trees are for planting in pots on balconies or patios.  Type B trees produce more

flowers but have to be planted in the ground.  A適合種在陽台.露台的盆栽裡、B會長更多的花

我想把植物種在屋子週圍,盆栽不是選項之一

W : Hmm, I want to plant them around the buildings.  Pots are not an option.  Do you deliver?

M : Of course, and we can also plant them for you for an additional $50 per tree.

我們也可以幫你種.一棵多50元

65. ( A )  Why does the woman want some trees?　改善這區域的外觀　但是要種在土裡(地)

　　(A)  To improve the appearance of an area.

　　(B)  To have a regular supply of flowers. 要固定供花　＊ produce

　　(C)  To conduct some scientific research. 執行科學研究　v.生產.製作

　　(D)  To provide more privacy for a home. 提供房屋隱私感　引起.

66. ( B )  Look at the graphic.  What size trees does the woman choose? 引走.

　　(A)  24 inches.　＊ supply　　＊ privacy　produce

　　(B)  36 inches.　　　　　　　　　　　　　　　　n.產品.農產品

　　(C)  48 inches.　v.供給.供應　　n.隱居.獨處.清靜

　　(D)  60 inches.　n.生活用品.補給品

| Magnolia Tree Size Chart | | | | |
|---|---|---|---|---|
| **Type** | **A** | **B** | **C** | **D** |
| **Height** | 24" | 36" | 48" | 60" |

67. ( C )  What additional service does the man offer the woman? ＊ harvest

　　(A)  Waste management. 廢棄物管理(垃圾處理) ① 收穫(雪) v.① 收割

　　(B)  Regular maintenance. 固定維修　　　　② 收成　　④ 得到

　　(C)  Tree planting. 種樹　　　　　　　　　③ 結果

　　(D)  Fruit harvesting. 收成水果

新的藥是30年研究的成果　　The new medicine is the harvest
of thirty years' research.

W : Mr. Greenberg. There's a conference that I'd like to attend in July and I'm wondering if the company would pay for it. The conference is on networking through social media, and I could learn a lot about how to reach a wider client base using social media.

M : I think that would be doable. We're always looking for ways to attract new clients. How much will it be?

W : I have the fee list here. You know, if I sign up today, I'll get the early registration discount.

M : Right... Um, why don't you go ahead and sign up? I'm curious to know what topics will be covered at the conference.

W : I've got all the information about times and topics. I'll send it to you in an e-mail.

68. ( C ) What department does the woman most likely work in?
   (A) Product development.
   (B) Information Technology.
   (C) Sales and Marketing.
   (D) Finance and Accounting.

69. ( C ) Look at the graphic. How much will the company most likely pay?
   (A) $1,700.
   (B) $2,200.
   (C) $2,300.
   (D) $2,900.

# NATIONAL NETWORKING CONFERNCE

## REGISTRATION FEES

|  | Early (before June 15) | Standard (after June 15) |
|---|---|---|
| Students | $1,700 | $2,200 |
| Professionals | $2,300 | $2,900 |

70. ( D ) What will the woman send the man in an e-mail?
   (A) A confirmation number.
   (B) A cashier's check.
   (C) A travel request form.
   (D) A conference schedule.

GO ON TO THE NEXT PAGE.

# PART 4

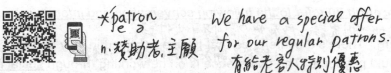

*patron* [ˈpetrən] n. 贊助者, 主顧

We have a special offer for our regular patrons. 有給老客人特別優惠

**Questions 71 through 73** *refer to the following excerpt from a seminar.*

歡迎來到今天的網路知識研討會, 我們很高興提供這次研討會給想增進線上經驗的 Tuscon 公共圖書館客戶們

Good afternoon and welcome to today's Internet literacy seminar. We are pleased to offer this seminar to all Tuscon Public Library patrons who want to improve their online experience. The library has recently purchased some new laptop computers here in the media center. And we're fortunate to have exclusive use of them today. Let's start our seminar by creating a user account for the TPL system—if you don't already have one. Your username will be the bar-code number which is found on the back of your card. For the password, however, please choose a word or phrase that you can easily remember.

圖書館最近買了些新電腦
在媒體中心
我們很幸運今天可以人專用這些電腦
你的使用者名稱會是你卡片背面的條碼
至於密碼, 嗯, 請選一個字或者詞組 你好記的

71. ( D )  What is the topic of the seminar?
    (A)  Computer programming. 電腦程式
    (B)  Graphic design. 平面設計
    (C)  Buying a used vehicle. 買台二手汽車
    (D)  Using the Internet. 用網路

*literature* n. 文學, 文學作品, 文獻
→ She went through the literature on the subject. 看過這個主題的所有文獻

*literacy* n. 識字, 能力, 知識

72. ( A )  What change did the library recently make? 圖書館最近有什麼改變
    (A)  It purchased new computers. 買新電腦
    (B)  It extended its hours. 時間延長
    (C)  It added a new media center. 增加新的媒體中心
    (D)  It reduced late fees. 減少延遲費

literacy level 某某文化水平
literacy skill 讀寫能力
computer literacy 電腦知識

73. ( C )  What are listeners asked to do?
    (A)  Apply for a card. 申請卡片
    (B)  Complete a survey. 完成調查
    (C)  Create an account. 創帳號
    (D)  Select a desktop theme. 選擇桌面主題

*literally* adv. 確實地, 名副其實地
→ We live literally just around the corner from her. 真的住離她很近

**Questions 74 through 76** *refer to the following telephone message.*

Hi, Ms. Chavez. This is Mike Renner calling from Amplify Communications. You've contracted us to set up a wireless network in your office, so your employees will have more flexible Internet access. However, according to the information you submitted to us, it looks like you have 30 employees scattered across two floors. The network we

fill make 放大, 增強, 擴張
聯絡 我們 了解 要 架設 網路 在你辦公室
所以你的員工會有 更有彈性的網路可使用
根據 你所提交的資訊
看起來你有30了個員工分散在二個樓層 adj. 散佈的, 散開的

agreed to install doesn't have enough bandwidth to accommodate that many simultaneous Internet users. Considering your tight budget, there are other network options that might work for you. So please give me a call and we can discuss them.

74. ( B ) Where does the speaker most likely work?
(A) At a fitness center.
(B) At a wireless network provider.
(C) At a paper supplier.
(D) At an office furniture store.

75. ( C ) What is the purpose of the message?
(A) To file a complaint.
(B) To offer an estimate.
(C) To suggest another service option.
(D) To ask for more time to complete a project.

76. ( C ) What does the speaker ask Ms. Chavez to do?
(A) Send a fax.
(B) Sign a contract.
(C) Return a phone call.
(D) Submit a deposit.

Questions 77 through 79 refer to the following telephone message.

Hello, Mr. Bailey. This is Marcel from D&T Farber. I'm calling about your personal income tax return. I think I may have figured out why the numbers weren't quite matching up. I found two deductions missing from your calculations, which I was able to fix relatively quickly. I'd like to meet with you in person though so that we can discuss the tax credit for which you are now eligible. I've already committed to helping other clients tomorrow but if you're free on Tuesday, I can stop by your office in the afternoon. Please call me back to let me know if that works for you. Thanks.

77. ( C ) Who most likely is the speaker?
(A) A court reporter.
(B) An architect.
(C) An accountant.
(D) A yoga instructor.

78. ( C ) What would the speaker like to discuss?
- (A) Reducing company spending. 減少,縮小公司開銷　reduce v. 減少
- (B) Utilizing office space effectively.　　　　　　　縮小
調整退稅 (C) Adjusting a tax return.　　有效地,實際上
adjust (D) Drafting a product proposal.　Effectively, their response was a
v.i 調整　　起草產品提案 ↑　　　　　　　refusal.

79. ( C ) What does the speaker say he will do tomorrow?　＊utilize
- (A) Take a vacation day. 休假　　　　　/jut!, əɪzɪ/ 利用
- (B) Attend a seminar. 參加研討會　＊adjust
- (C) Meet with clients. 和客戶見面　v.i 調整.校正
- (D) Mail some forms. 寄送一些表格　I must adjust my watch, it's fast.
She must learn to adjust herself

**Questions 80 through 82** refer to the following announcement. to English life.

剛才品管部跟我說我們今早組裝的腳踏車
Hey, guys. We just got word from quality assurance that there are some issues with
不直有些彎曲(bent)　　有些問題(下)
the bikes we assembled this morning. The frames are slightly bent. It seems to be a
一個貨柜裡有一些數量有問題　　　　　　　　所以我們已經找人
problem with a limited number of frames in one shipment, so we've got someone taking
丈量這批貨　批　　　那明顯地我們無法正常運作直到這個問題解決
measurements on the lot. We are obviously unable to operate normally until this
而且現在正好是午餐時間　　因此,我們會提早休息
problem is resolved and it's just about lunch time. Therefore, we'll break early and
並多休小時　　　當回到生產樓層時
take an extra hour. When we come back down on the production floor at 2:00 p.m.,
　　　　　　　　(下)
we'll hopefully be able to carry on as usual.
希望可以如同以往繼續進行　　　＊bent adj. 彎曲的
　　　　　　　　　　　　　　　　　n. 愛好: He has a bent
80. ( D ) Where is this announcement most likely being made?　　　　for art.
- (A) At an art gallery. 在畫廊　　　＊warehouse
- (B) At a department store. 在百貨公司　五金行.倉庫.批發店.大型零售店
- (C) At an appliance warehouse. 在電器五金行
- (D) At a bicycle factory. 腳踏車工廠　＊carry on

81. ( B ) What problem does the speaker mention? → He does carry on, doesn't he?
有些客戶抱怨 (A) Some customers have complained. 他有點胡鬧.對吧!
有些素材不完美 (B) Some materials are faulty. 有缺點的 → Carry on the rising cost of living.
- (C) A shipment has not arrived. 不美美的　一直嚷嚷不休說生活成本提高
- (D) A business has opened late.
有間店開到很晚　　　　　　→ (D)
82. ( C ) What are the listeners told to do?　It's said the secretary is carrying
- (A) Come in early tomorrow. 明天早點來 on with her boss.
- (B) Print more copies of a flyer. 列多一點傳單
- (C) Take a longer lunch break. 午休長一點　不當男女關係
- (D) Contact a manager.
聯絡經理

62

會議結束之前再做最後一個宣佈　　我想告訴你關於我們其中一個

One last announcement before we close the meeting. I'd like to tell you about a new

同事組織的資主募款活動

fundraiser that's being organized by one of our co-workers, Lee Van Vliet. After

在知道我們當地社區中心有需要募款(資主)　　他決定用募款來幫忙

learning that our local community center was in need of funding, Lee decided to help

又有這週，捐出捐會被放在自助餐廳

out by raising some money. So this week only, a donation box will be placed in the

你願意給的任何金額都非常感謝

cafeteria during lunch. And any amount that you're willing to give will be greatly

會請代表人員來參加下去會議，談論資主將會如何使用在

appreciated. Lee has asked the representative from the community center to come

to our next meeting to talk about how funds will be used to benefit the center. 福利中心

83. ( A ) What does the speaker ask the listeners to participate in?
- (A) A fund-raising activity. 募款活動
- (B) A company picnic. 公司野餐　　n. 津貼.利益.好處n
- (C) A training workshop. 訓練課程　　v. 有益於
- (D) A community art festival. 社區藝術節　　The mountain air will benefit you.

84. ( C ) What will be available in the cafeteria this week? * attendance
- (A) Healthy menu choices. 健康菜單
- (B) Special desserts. 特製甜點　　n 到場 出席
- (C) A donation box. 捐獻箱　　→ My attendance at school is excellent.
- (D) A sign-up sheet. 報名表　　護理,伺候

85. ( D ) What does the speaker say about the next meeting? → She is in attendance
- (A) New employees will be introduced. 介紹新員工　　on the sick child.
- (B) Attendance will be required. 會要求出席率　　在照顧生病的小孩
- (C) It will be in a different location. 會在不同的地點
- (D) A guest will speak. 貴客會演講

not down end
* indefinitely
adv. 無期限地
模糊地　　他表達的不太清楚

She expressed herself rather indefinitely.

This morning, another regional hospital announced that it will be closing its mobile

行動診所是設計來改善

health clinic indefinitely. The mobile clinic was designed to improve access to quality

佳在郊區 城市以外區域的人擁有 有品質醫療照顧而取得

health care for people living in the rural areas outside of the city. According to a

根據發言人　　醫院執行行動診所10年3直到

spokesperson, the hospital ran a mobile health clinic for ten years until forced to shut

因為有問題被迫停止　　因為使醫所護的預算整個國家到被削減

it down because of budget cutbacks. As budgets for health care are being slashed

across the state, authorities are concerned about rural health care, as fewer people

will have access to quality services. 當局很擔心郊區的健照狀況

國家,國土,州(大盛),地位　　更少對入能接觸到有品質的服務

The superstar lives in state. 過著豪華的生活

GO ON TO THE NEXT PAGE.

86. ( C ) According to the news report, what type of facility is being closed?
    (A) A vocational school.
    (B) A bus station.
    (C) A medical clinic. 診所
    (D) A community center. 社區中心

什麼地方要被關閉 場所.地點.廁所

#eliminate
out 剔除
v.排除.消滅
淘汰

Our goal is to eliminate poverty.

→ Our team was eliminated from the competition in the first round.

87. ( C ) Why was the facility closed?
    (A) It was outdated. 過時的
    (B) Its program was not popular. 節目.課程不受歡迎
    (C) Its funding was eliminated. 資金被刪除.消減
    (D) It was in a remote location.

根據報導,當局擔心日後會發生什麼?是在遠遠的地點

88. ( A ) According to the news report, what do authorities fear will happen in the future?
*lack 缺少
I don't seem to lack anything.
    (A) More people will lack adequate health care. 缺乏足夠的健康照護
    (B) Public transportation will improve. 改善公眾運輸
    (C) The income of rural workers will increase. 郊區工作者的收入增加
    (D) Similar services will open in other areas.

類似的服務會在別區開始

'adequate adj.足夠的 (上)
to equi
equal
適當的
尚可的

**Questions 89 through 91** refer to the following advertisement.

專門在做傳統的西里島食物

Looking for an Italian restaurant that specializes in traditional Sicilian foods? Then
come visit us at Trattoria di Palermo opening soon on West Pico Blvd. Our menu
features the famous Sicilian cuisine. All of our unique dishes are prepared from
recipes passed down for generations. The restaurant's opening celebration will take
place on October 10 from 5:00 p.m. to 10:00 p.m. There'll be food samples and live
music. The first 50 guests will be given a free laminated map of Sicily with the Trattoria
di Palermo logo. For more information, visit our website at www.trattoriadipalermo.com.

以~為特色
boulevard / bulə)vard/
我們所有的特色美
習足一代代傳下來的食譜
開幕慶祝活動
食品樣電
現場
音樂表演
層層壓的地圖

89. ( C ) What is special about the restaurant?
    (A) Its location.
    (B) Its service.
    (C) Its food.
    (D) Its design.

The hotel is merely 'adequate. 飯店還OK

He sought for an adequate solution to the problem.
seek - sought - sought 找適當的解決方法

90. ( A ) According to the speaker, what will happen on October 10?
    (A) A grand opening will take place. 盛大開幕
    (B) A major renovation will start. 大規模整修
    (C) A new chef will start work. 新廚開始工作
    (D) A cooking class will be offered. 有烹飪課

* major adj.較大的.較多的
主要的.一流的
* renovation n.更新.修理
* grand adj.盛大的.偉大的
華麗的

91. ( D ) What will some guests receive?
    (A) Memberships.
    (B) Calendars.
    (C) T-shirts.
    (D) Maps.

**Questions 92 through 94** refer to the following speech.

You all deserve a big round of applause today for your hard work in developing the advertising campaign for our longtime client, Pointier Hotel Group. This campaign introducing the group's new chain of boutique hotels was very innovative. For the first time, we created advertisements on social networking sites as well. The ads we created for these sites were particularly effective. Pointier has reported that online bookings have increased by 200% since the campaign started. This indicates that people are reading the online ads and following the website link to learn more about staying in one of their hotels. Our clients are thrilled about this increase, and so am I. Thank you to the entire team for your continued contributions to our company's success.

92. ( B ) What type of business was the advertising campaign designed for?
    (A) A bank.
    (B) A hotel group.
    (C) A real estate agency.
    (D) A restaurant chain.

93. ( C ) According to the speaker, what was different about the advertising campaign?
    (A) A celebrity was hired to endorse a product.
    (B) A promotional period was extended.
    (C) Ads were posted on social networking sites.
    (D) Coupons were sent by mobile phone.

94. ( D ) According to the speaker, what indicates that the advertising campaign was a success?
    (A) Positive survey results
    (B) Product sample requests
    (C) Increased foot traffic in retail.
    (D) More website bookings.

GO ON TO THE NEXT PAGE.

**Questions 95 through 97** *refer to the following broadcast and schedule.*

你現在的頻道是KTJB電台. 我們最新的當地新聞. 市議會昨天通過商業區路燈改善的預算

You're tuned to KTJB radio. In our last local news story of the hour, the Stanton city council met yesterday to approve a budget for street light improvements in the city's 廣告區. 商業區

commercial area. 市商裡的老闆們一直要求 市府 可以在市中心多裝 200支路燈 City business owners have been petitioning the city council for the 過去這兩年以來

past two years to install 200 additional streetlights in the downtown area. 他們相信更好的火光光會鼓勵商人在夜之後可生意 They believe that the better lighting will encourage business after dark. In an interview this morning,

city council president Robert Miller reported that the estimated cost of the street lights

will be about five hundred thousand dollars.

在早上的面談中, 市議會長 (市長)
說, 預估路燈的費用大概是
500,000 元.

廣播的目的 (指) 為何?

95. ( D )  What is the purpose of the broadcast?
   (A) To advertise a store opening.
   (B) To report traffic conditions. 報導交通狀況
   (C) To remind listeners of an election. 提醒聽眾有選舉
   (D) To announce a city council decision. 宣佈市府的決定

* petition /pə'tɪʃən/
V 向~請願, 請求, 要求
n. 請願(書), 訴求, 申請

96. ( B )  What did local business owners request?
   (A) A new parking structure. 新的停車建築
   (B) Additional street lights. 多的路燈
   (C) An alternate date for an event. 活動要改日期
   (D) An advertising campaign. 廣告宣傳活動

* alternate adj. 不同的 change

97. ( D )  Look at the graphic. What will the speaker most likely talk about next?
   (A) Today's top headlines. 今日頭條
   (B) The estimated cost of a construction project. 建設案的預估花費
   (C) Names of newly elected officials. 新選出來的政府頭
   (D) Traffic conditions. 交通狀況

* tune
n. 曲調, 旋律, 語氣
→ The piano is out of tune. 鋼琴走調了
②協調 → A person out of tune with his surroundings is unhappy. 一致
③正常的狀態 (心情)
Are you in tune for study today? 你今天有心情唸書嗎?

**KTJB Morning Schedule**
**(9:15-10:00)**

| | |
|---|---|
| 9:15 | Headline news |
| 9:20 | Business report |
| 9:30 | Local news |
| 9:35 | Traffic update |

tune
④為~調音, 調整 → The machine has just been tuned.
調~頻道              機器剛調整過

**66**

*Questions 98 through 100* refer to the following telephone message and agenda.

我本來明天早上該和銷售代表們見面,告訴他們價格改變的內容

Hi, Joseph. This is Maureen. I'm supposed to meet with our sales representatives tomorrow morning and give them a presentation about the changes in our pricing.

但不幸的是 我覺得不舒服,而且我不曉得我明天可以去到公室 所以我在想你是否可以代替我

But unfortunately, I'm not feeling well and I don't think I'll be able to make it to the office tomorrow. So, I was wondering if you would mind taking over for me. I just e-mailed you the slides and notes for the presentation. Feel free to call me with any questions after you have a look at the attachments. Thank you so much.

看完附件後有任何問題請打給我. 謝謝.

98. ( C ) Why is the woman unable to come to the office tomorrow?
    (A) She will be at a conference. 參加會議    *take over
    (B) She has a sales appointment. 銷售會議    接管.繼任
    (C) She is feeling ill. 覺得不舒服    * ill
    (D) She is expecting visitors. 在等拜訪者   n. 生病的.壞的    急速地
    → Ill news runs apace.

99. ( A ) What does the woman ask Joseph to do?
    (A) Give a presentation. 做報告    adv. 壞地.困難地
    (B) Postpone an event. 活動延期    → She was ill treated.
    (C) Verify some prices. 核實.查證一些價格   I can ill afford the time.
    (D) Consult a colleague. 咨詢同事    我花不起這個時間

100. ( C ) Please look at the graphic. In what order will Joseph give a presentation at the meeting?
    (A) First.   * outlook     n. 不幸.禍害.苦腦
    (B) Second.   n.展望.前景.景色.風光   → Who can cure the economic
    (C) Third.   注視.瞭望      ills?
    (D) Fourth.      * verify

v.核實.證明.查實
The truth verified the allegations.

allegation
æ ə e

n.陳述.宣稱.主張 辯解.指控

```
┌─────────────────────────────────────────┐
│      Sales Representative Meeting Agenda →│
│   開場                                     │
│      Opening talk — Jeff                  │
│ 行銷預算  Marketing budget — Harry         │
│ 價格增加 Price increases — Maureen         │
│ 季的展望 Quarterly outlook — Diane         │
└─────────────────────────────────────────┘
```

GO ON TO THE NEXT PAGE.

# READING TEST

In the Reading test, you will read a variety of texts and answer several different types of reading comprehension questions. The entire Reading test will last 75 minutes. There are three parts, and directions are given for each part. You are encouraged to answer as many questions as possible within the time allowed.

You must mark your answers on the separate answer sheet. Do not write your answers in your test book.

## PART 5

**Directions**: A word or phrase is missing in each of the sentences below. Four answer choices are given below each sentence. Select the best answer to complete the sentence. Then mark the letter (A), (B), (C), or (D) on your answer sheet.

101. This West Lake Avenue entrance will be closed until ------- on the parking garage has been completed.
(A) constructs
(B) construction
(C) constructed
(D) constructive

102. Glover Foods, Inc. ------- yesterday that it expects diminished revenue growth over the next year.
(A) announced
(B) has announced
(C) announces
(D) announcing

103. The legal documents that Ms. Lavery needs are on file ------- the county courthouse.
(A) above
(B) after
(C) at
(D) among

104. Axion's new line of electric vehicles features ------- exterior designs and advanced battery technology.
(A) attractive
(B) attracting
(C) attract
(D) attraction

105. The Pancake House is as popular ------- Walter's Diner in the southern parts of the city.
(A) either
(B) with
(C) as
(D) of

106. When Everest Outdoor Apparel has a surplus of certain items, the company ------- donates the items to local charities.
(A) regularities
(B) regularly
(C) regularize
(D) regularity

107. The candidate we select must be able to work effectively ------- alone and in group situations.
(A) the same as
(B) not only
(C) also
(D) both

108. Quartz Light Speed sales representatives are reminded to follow specific ------- even when servicing regular customers.
(A) guidelines
(B) behaviors
(C) records
(D) qualifications

109. For ------- printing quality, use compatible Icer inkjet cartridges.
(A) optimally
(B) optimizing
(C) optimal
(D) optimize

110. The company president ------- Ms. Iverson with securing the contract with Star General Motors.
(A) agreed
(B) congratulated
(C) demonstrated
(D) entrusted

111. Mr. Simon said that to finish the contract proposal on time, ------- must volunteer to stay late tonight.
(A) one another
(B) anyone
(C) no one
(D) someone

112. Ms. Walker ------- sold the benefits of her expansion plan, winning the support of the company's executive board.
(A) convincingly
(B) convincing
(C) convinces
(D) convince

113. *Radiate Monthly Digest* features news from companies ------- the alternative energy industry.
(A) onto
(B) next
(C) in
(D) during

114. The growth of Tyrus Industrial Corp. over the past three quarters has failed to meet shareholders' -------.
(A) expectations
(B) expectedly
(C) expect
(D) expected

115. Food producers are experiencing high demand for ------- soy-based products.
(A) themselves
(B) them
(C) they
(D) their

116. The oversight committee will be limited to seven members so that the group may follow its agenda more -------.
(A) efficiencies
(B) efficiently
(C) efficient
(D) efficiency

117. Hotel employees will be happy to ------- guests seeking a nearby restaurant or movie theater.
(A) locate
(B) conduct
(C) assist
(D) remind

118. Job candidates have been cautioned that the interview process is highly ------- and only two positions will be filled.
(A) competition
(B) competitive
(C) competitors
(D) competitively

119. The self-recharging nickel ion battery is the ------- of many years of intensive research and experimentation.
(A) product
(B) producer
(C) produced
(D) producing

120. Sales of Crager Lawn Chief riding mowers increase ------- during the spring and summer seasons.
(A) openly
(B) rigidly
(C) dramatically
(D) frequently

GO ON TO THE NEXT PAGE.

**121.** All employees are invited to ~~attend~~ the reception banquet at 7:30 p.m. in the Biltmore Ballroom of the Royal Terrace Hotel. 接待晚宴

(A) express
(B) admit
(C) perform
(D) attend

*[手寫] D / attend / 名詞片語 / 限定詞 + adj. + 名詞 / threatened with*

**122.** Cory Fountain is the ------- president of Star Steel Industries in the history of the company. 有史以來最大膽的總裁

(A) boldness
(B) bolder
(C) boldest → She was hurt by his bold remark.
(D) boldly

*[手寫] C / *bold adj. 英勇的、寬長的、大膽的*

**123.** Before recommending investments to clients, financial consultants at Barron Stone consider ------- variables such as age, occupation, and income. 在給客戶建議的投資選項前，財務顧問會

(A) quantified 使量化
(B) specific 特定的
(C) occupied 佔用的
(D) accountable 應負責任的

*[手寫] B / 考量特定變因、如年齡、職業和收入 / be accountable for 對~負責任*

**124.** Patients who cancel appointments without 24-hour advance notice are subject to a $50 cancellation fee. 受~控制、有一傾向

(A) usually adv.
(B) already adv.
(C) without 介, adv.
(D) almost adv.

*[手寫] C / The party is subject to government supervision. 這個政党受政府控管、監督. / The country is subject to earth-quakes. 常遭受地震.*

**125.** All staff members are asked to shut down their computers when ------- the office to conserve energy. 傳達、傳送

(A) exit 所有員工被要求關閉電腦當離開
(B) exits 辦公室的時候，為了節省能源
(C) exited
(D) exiting 'exit 介. 離開 → exiting 動v. 當 S, n. 出口

*[手寫] D*

**126.** Although the ------- findings did not prove the fabric to be water-resistant, the later results did. 雖然一開始的研究發現並未證明布料是防水的，之後的

(A) initial
(B) present
(C) forward 結果有. *fabric ⑩ 布料 ⑩ 結構
(D) ahead → The whole social fabric was disintegration. 社會結構有瓦解的危險

*[手寫] A*

**127.** After attending a recent sculpture ------- at The Wyatt Museum, Derek Logan signed up for an introductory art course offered by the museum. 參加最近的雕刻

(A) portrait 肖像、排行
(B) creativity 創造力
(C) exhibition
(D) message 消息

*[手寫] C / 展之後，他報名了堂博物館開的初級藝術課.*

**128.** Photo identification is required for all non-authorized visitors to the Blight Building. 有照片的身分證明是需要的，

(A) for
(B) which
(C) until require 書及物用時 → 需要
(D) despite The roof requires repairing. The project will require less money.

*[手寫] A / 所有未授權的拜訪者.*

**129.** The Ardos operating system from Bridge Solutions will ------- users to automate numerous repetitive tasks.

(A) show Ardos 操作系統會讓使用者們
(B) allow
(C) avoid 自動化很多車複的任務 (動作)
(D) provide (可以節省時間)

*[手寫] B*

**130.** Six people from the marketing and public relations departments at Stabb Creative are being considered for ------- to management positions. 6位來自了銷和公

(A) transmission 開部門的人被列為晉升管理
(B) openings
(C) advancement 職位的考量人選
(D) opportunities

*[手寫] C / → 進展、晉升、發展 / 預付款項 / 開始、開幕、職缺、機會 / Good openings for business.*

## PART 6

**Directions**: Read the texts that follow. A word, phrase, or sentence is missing in parts of each text. Four answer choices are given below each of the texts. Select the best answer to complete the text. Then mark the letter (A), (B), (C), or (D) on your answer sheet.

Questions 131-134 refer to the following advertisement.

Top Notch Landscaping

Top Notch designs and installs landscapes with all types of plants, using all natural materials to suit every garden no matter how big or small. Our designs have ------- modest urban gardens as well

**131.**

as large-scale projects commissioned by architects and property developers. -------. However, no single nursery can offer plants of

**132.**

all species and varieties. That is why Top Notch has developed

close relationships with specialty growers who ------- provide us

**133.**

with the plants we need. Such resources give us the selection

necessary to complete any -------. In other words, whatever your

**134.**

landscaping goals may be, we can make it happen.

**131.** (A) collected
(B) planted
(C) transformed
(D) distributed

**132.** (A) We are here to solve your home renovation problems
(B) For most projects, we use plants and materials sourced from our own nurseries
(C) Some cities have specific usage ordinances
(D) Under normal conditions, nursery stock is guaranteed for 30 days

**133.** (A) readiness
(B) readies
(C) readily
(D) ready

**134.** (A) project
(B) survey
(C) study
(D) form

*[Handwritten annotations present throughout, including: "* modest 謙虛的、端莊的、適度的", "Prices tended to rise year by year, but at a modest rate.", "She is wearing a modest bathing suit.", "* collect 收集、採集、接", "→ He has gone to collect his daughter.", "受話人付費 You can call me collect.", "* readily 輕易地、立刻地、無困難地", "→ She answers readily when called on.", "→ Laptops are readily available these days."]*

*dedication（意有處於對方之下）
down | say 奉獻 致力
tell He dedicated his life to science.
The school dedicated the new building
on Sunday. 落成典禮

| To: | Staff |
|---|---|
| From: | Lou Swift |
| Date: | April 5 |
| Subject: | Big News! |

Dear Staff,

謝謝你們的付出和團隊合作.            以防你們還不知道這個大消息
Thanks for your dedication and teamwork! In case you haven't

heard the big news, Swifty Lube will be ~~opening~~ a new location this

今年夏天會開新地點! 這個新的服務中心正在   135. 施工當中
summer. This additional service center is currently under

construction at the corner of Geary Street and Park Presidio Drive

in the Richmond District of San Francisco.

我們會開始收符合資格的 汽車技術人員和銷售人員申請. 直到 6月1號
We will be accepting applications for qualified auto technicians and

sales positions ------- June 1. Paul Grisham, our hiring director, will
            136.

personally review applicants' qualifications from June 2 to June 9,

and ------- is scheduled to begin one week later. -------.
      137.                              138.

Paul, 我們的雇用主管會親自審查
申請者的資格 從 6/2～6/9

Cheers,

Lou Swift, CEO  然後訓練預計在一周後開始, 歡迎分享告知這個機會.
Swifty Lube

如果你還在等預約請聯絡 Swifty Lube

expose 暴露

**135.** (A) exposing
B (B) opening
    (C) moving
    (D) changing

去大門的入口會因建設
而有阻礙 C
（做路所以不通）

**136.** (A) according to
C (B) with
    (C) until
    (D) following

歡迎和有興趣的朋
以及家人分享這個消息
（機會）

**137.** (A) trainer e
B (B) training
    (C) trains
    (D) trained

**138.** (A) Contact Swifty Lube if you are still waiting for an appointment
    (B) Access to the <u>main entrance</u> will be blocked by construction
    (C) Feel free to share this opportunity with interested friends and family
    (D) Make sure you have received all of the training materials before proceeding

在進行以前請確認有收到全部的
訓練資料.
*proceeding 在3. 學會的會議. 活動記錄.
→ The proceedings were published in the newspaper.

Smith-Tyler Donates to Youth Center in Nashville

A spokesperson for Jabari Smith-Tyler ------- that the basketball
139.

star made a sizeable donation toward the expansion of the West
Nashville Youth and Recreation Center. "Without his generous
support," said Ibn Ali, director of the center, "we would have
been thwarted in our renovation plans going forward."

-------.  Now, a new wing will be constructed on the north end of
140.

the ------- gymnasium.  The building will boast an Olympic-sized
141.

swimming pool, state-of-the-art indoor tennis courts, and new
staff and administrative offices.  Additionally, private locker
rooms will be located ------- the current youth lounge.
142.

139. (A) has confirmed
(B) will confirm
(C) confirming
(D) confirmation

140. (A) Youth Center attendance has decreased
over the past few years
(B) The original swimming pool is being
converted into a game room
(C) Mr. Jabari's performance at the gymnasium
was outstanding
(D) The project had been delayed because of
budget cuts

141. (A) scheduled
(B) proposed
(C) irritable
(D) existing

142. (A) instead of
(B) as far as
(C) adjacent to
(D) even though

GO ON TO THE NEXT PAGE.

19

*console* v. 安慰
/kən'soʊl/ she consoled him with soft words.
/kɒnsoʊl/ n. 操作台, 落地TV, Radio

Date: August 4
To: Daria Steller <daria@coolmail.com>
From: Hugh Lomax <hlomax@wixler.com>
Subject: Product recall 產品召回

Dear Ms. Steller,

Thank you for your recent ------- of the Wixler Fire TV Gaming Edition *purchase*
(143.) Console. We are contacting everyone who has recently bought this
正在聯絡最近有買這 一項產品的人, 通知他們一些特定的型號被召回 維修
product to inform them that certain models are being recalled for
repair. 在這些型號裡, 8署類比訊號(錄音帶)轉換成數位訊號的處理器 壞掉了(有缺點的) AD(→輸入→廠裡→ DAS→播出
In these models, the processor that enables the digital conversion

of analog signal is faulty. -------. Please ------- whether your console
144.    145.
請看編號確認你的操作器是否有問題, 如果開頭是087, 需要被維修
has this problem by checking the serial number on the bottom of the

unit. If it begins with the numbers "087," a repair will be required.

Wixler will pay all shipping costs for sending your Fire TV back to
所有運送費用由Wixler支付
us. In addition, we will repair it free ------- charge. 小缺點
146.    *of*

Thank you, 除此之外, 我們是免費維修的
flaw       imperfection
fault      deficiency
Hugh Lomax, Customer Service Manager
shortcoming  weakness
Wixler Industries
blemish    foible 性格的
           /fɔːrbl/ 小缺點

(A) 這個缺點最終會扭曲
    說喇叭出來的聲音        n. 確認 *verify

143. (A) response 回應          145. (A) verification true
 C   (B) demonstration 展示       C   (B) verified v. 證明
     (C) purchase 購買              (C) verify
     (D) review                     (D) verifies *verily*
         評論    ─ 缺點(E)                    又名
144. (A) This defect will eventually distort the sound   146. (A) at  adv. 真正地, 真實地
 A       coming from the speakers   →twist 扭曲   B   (B) of
     (B) This special feature is unavailable on some       (C) with  *verdict*
         older models 這個特殊功能在一些老舊的型號上   (D) on
     (C) We hope you will enjoy your new home for         n. 判決, 判斷
         many years to come = for many more years 無法使用.
     (D) It is covered in the troubleshooting section  →希望你接下來這幾年都能愛
         of the manual 手冊裡的疑難排解區有說          你的新家

# PART 7

**Directions**: In this part you will read a selection of texts, such as magazine and newspaper articles, e-mails, and instant messages. Each text or set of texts is followed by several questions. Select the best answer for each question and mark the letter (A), (B), (C), or (D) on your answer sheet.

**Questions 147-148** refer to the following advertisement.

※和天氣相關資訊
降雨機率 probability of precipitation
潮位 water level
潮高 tidal height
high tide ↔ low tide

## Storm King Windows

訂製的替換窗戶，為亞熱帶和大陸型氣候設計的
Custom-fitted replacement windows designed

for subtropical and continental climates
大陸的 (什麼都有)
continent
n. 洲、大陸地

Serving Residential and Commercial Needs
服務住家和商務用途 ※相對濕度 relative humidity
能見度 visibility
Free estimates
陣雨 rain shower

Visit our showroom at: 447 Holly Street, Cedar Rapids, IA 66720

Monday through Saturday, 10:00 A.M.-6:00 P.M.

Joseph Kalani      ※氣壓計 barometer          海嘯 tsunami
Product Consultant   氣候學 climatology         颱風 typhoon
                     即時預報 nowcasting        天氣圖 weather chart

劇烈天氣 severe weather   餘震 aftershock
熱帶氣旋 tropical cyclone

他在什麼領域工作?
**147.** In what field is Mr. Kalani employed?
(D)
  (A) Insurance. 保險
  (B) Cleaning and maintenance. 清潔維護
  (C) Commercial advertising. 廣告
  (D) Retail sales. 零售

**148.** What is indicated about Storm King Windows? 僱用新的技術人員
(C)
  (A) It is hiring new technicians.
  (B) It has just renovated a showroom. 剛整修一間展示室
  (C) It serves homeowners and businesses.
  (D) It has just moved to Holly Street.

*GO ON TO THE NEXT PAGE.*

### ■ ■ ■ ■ Attention Library Users ■ ■ ■ ■

The current Book-a-Book on-site reservation process will no longer be available at the Fairhaven City Library as of October 1. We will be transitioning to a new online Book-a-Book system that will allow patrons to reserve library materials remotely from their own computers. The new system will be unveiled in mid-September.

Any requests for items in the current Book-a-Book system made before October 1 will be honored. However, these requests will not appear in the new system. As of October 1, any questions about the status of reservations made through the old system should be directed to a librarian.

We appreciate your patience during the transition period.

149. What is the purpose of the announcement?
(A) To attract new readers.
(B) To give notice of changes to a procedure.
(C) To invite patrons to an event at the library.
(D) To introduce a new staff member.

150. What will happen to existing reservations after October 1?
(A) They will be canceled.
(B) They will no longer be free.
(C) They will be viewable only by librarians.
(D) They will need to be reconfirmed by patrons.

**Questions 151-152** refer to the following text-message chain. ＊ripe adj. 成熟的
1ㄞ1

---

**Doug Gleason (12:32 P.M.)**     1. The corn is ripe.

我們剛收到一個從 Equi Farm 來的小黃瓜貨。 2. He is ripe in judgement.

Hi Kim. We just received a shipment of cucumbers from Equi Farms. Should I place the new cucumbers on top of our current stock? Or should I sort them so that the riper ones are in front?

我該把新的小黃瓜放在我們存貨的最上面嗎？或者我應該把牠分類一下(分類一下)
所以較熟的放在比較前面呢？

**Kim Pignato (12:35 P.M.)**
多謝詢問，我們通常會重新安排
Thanks for checking. We usually rearrange them. Ask Sara to show you how.

問Sara教你怎麼用

2. 有成熟的判斷力
3. The time is ripe for a new foreign policy.

**Doug Gleason (12:36 P.M.)**   採用新外交政策時機已成熟

Got it. One more thing. Fuji apples are on sale this week. We may need to order more. 富士蘋果這週在特價，我們需要訂多一點貨

**Kim Pignato (12:37 P.M.)** 當這周繼續前進(這周晚一點)，我們會持續
紀錄，了解~的動態  了解特價的狀況
We'll keep track of sales and decide as the week goes on.

**Doug Gleason (12:39 P.M.)**
(A)重新安排小黃瓜的展示
//Sounds good.// 聽起來不錯哦！  (B)請Sara聯絡Pignato
(C)用優惠價賣富士蘋果
(D)需要的話再下另一筆訂單

---

**151.** Who most likely is Ms. Pignato?
C  (A) A server. 服務員
(B) A farmer. 農夫
(C) A store manager. 店經理
(D) A food distributor. 食物經銷商·批發商

**152.** At 12:39 P.M., what does Mr. Gleason
D  agree to do when he writes, //"Sounds good."//?
(A) Rearranging the cucumber display.
(B) Asking Sara to contact Ms. Pignato.
(C) Selling Fuji apples at a discount.
(D) Placing another order only if needed.

GO ON TO THE NEXT PAGE.

*obligation n. 義務  promote v. 促使 adj. 即時的  *pilot n. 飛行員 adj. 試驗的  a pilot farm
a 一area 一  促使  迅速的                                                        plant
                                                                            production

## Starlight Industries Pairs Up with E&T Recycling Center

Starlight 電腦科技公司剛宣佈了將會和E&T回收中心合作

June 19—The computer technology company Starlight Industries just announced it will begin working with E&T Recycling Centers. This partnership will enable

這次合作能夠讓消費者可免費(安心的)回收電腦設備

consumers to responsibly recycle computer equipment, at no personal cost, simply by taking it to a collection center.

└需任何個人開支.只要帶去回收中心即可/用過的電腦造成廢棄物來源快速的

"Used computers make up a rapidly growing waste 增加 source," said CEO Indira Kapoor. "As a major producer of

即使電腦商品的主要生產者,我相信

computer products, we believe it is our obligation to reuse

這是我們的義務來重新使用可利用的並讓重金屬遠離

what we can and keep heavy metals out of the landfills.

This is what prompted us to go forward with this initiative." 垃圾場

這就是促使我們開始做這件事情的原因 →一開始只支持2個試做的回收場

Starlight Industries originally sponsored two pilot E&T

有鑑於那2個的成功.目標要增加10個場地,在年底時

collection sites and, given their success, aims to add ten more sites by year's end. To learn more about the initiative and for a map of current and proposed collection sites, visit ETrecyclingcenter.com.

我想知道更多有關這個活動和目前及未來可能的回收地點.請上網站.

*responsibly
adv. 負責地.可信賴地.認真負責地

153. According to Ms. Kapoor, why did her company partner with a recycling firm?
C
(A) To manufacture more affordable computer products 生產更多負擔得起的電腦產
(B) To follow a government environmental policy. 跟隨政府環境政策品
(C) To meet a responsibility as an industry leader. 身為行業領導的責任
(D) To pursue a rewarding financial opportunity. follow
追求一個有報酬的財務機會  *rewarding 有報酬的.有利益的

154. What is stated about collection sites?
D
(A) They are not getting as much use as expected. 不如預期的大量使用
(B) They are no longer accepting volunteers. 不再收志願者
(C) Their sanitary requirements are very strict. 衛生要求非常嚴格
(D) Their locations can be found on an online map. 線上地圖可以找到地點。

**Questions 155-157** refer to the following article.

Chef and lifestyle coach Lana Watson has announced her first foray into cosmetics with the launch of a new skin care business. Her Summer Garden skin care line consists solely of products made from organic ingredients and features extracts from plants, fruits, and vegetables. — [1] —.

"I've always served the healthiest possible food in my restaurant," said Ms. Watson. "Natural ingredients nourish our health and beauty from the inside out.

— [2] —. My skin care line utilizes only the vitamins and proteins in foods, such as spinach and cucumber, and combines them to create powerful moisturizers and cleansers that are free from artificial chemicals. — [3] —."

Summer Garden products are suitable for those with dry, sensitive, or combination skin and will be available online and at select retail stores beginning this September. — [4] —.

**155.** What is the article mainly about?

(A) Local organic farms.
(B) Online shopping trends.
(C) A new business venture.
(D) A company merger.

**156.** What is indicated about Summer Garden products?

(A) They are suitable for all ages.
(B) They are available for purchase now.
(C) They are relatively inexpensive.
(D) They contain no artificial ingredients.

**157.** In which of the positions marked [1], [2], [3], and [4] does the following sentence best belong?

"It seemed logical to create the products to nurture our skin from the outside in."

(A) [1].
(B) [2].
(C) [3].
(D) [4].

GO ON TO THE NEXT PAGE.

*override v. 願忽視, 推翻
He overrides his friend's advice.
He was demoted for overriding his supervisor's orders.
無視吾官命令被降職了

| To: | Department Managers |
|---|---|
| From: | Margaret Langley |
| Date: | December 27 |
| Subject: | Extended absence greeting |
| Attachment: | Sample message #5 |

語訊錄問候語 (Voice mail) greetings

Dear Managers,

In preparation for the upcoming holiday, when offices will be closed, I'd like to remind you that company policy requires each of our departments to replace the traditional greeting on their voice messaging systems with an extended-absence greeting that will play next week when callers are diverted to voice mail. This will involve making a new recording, saving it to the system, and programming the system to activate the recording at the close of our business day on Friday. Once you activate the extended-absence greeting, it will override the traditional greeting through the holiday.

The attached document contains the text of the greeting you should record. This is the same text we have used in the past, but as usual, the dates have been changed to reflect the current closure. Please use this document to record your holiday greeting. Make sure you activate it before you leave for the day on Friday.

158. What is the subject of the e-mail?

(A) A newly established company policy. 新成立的公司政策

(B) An improved way to access voice mail. 進入語音信箱的新方法

(C) A procedure related to a holiday closing. 和假日關門相關的

(D) A change to the traditional shift schedule. 傳統的輪班行程表改變

159. What is included as an attachment?

(A) A script to be read aloud.

(B) A flyer announcing a company event.

(C) Instructions for installing a new phone.

(D) Transcripts of recorded customer calls.

160. What is indicated in the e-mail about the attached document?

(A) It is ready for publication.

(B) It is distributed annually. 一年一次

(C) It is handed out to customers.

(D) It is intended only for new employees.

intend for 為~而準備
又適合用於新員工

Questions 161-163 refer to the following article.

**Around Town**

*By Charmaine Snyder*

(August 10)—Robbin's has been a fixture on Bennington Street for over 80 years. The department store also served as Frederick Atkinson's entry into the working world when he was a teenager.

For three years, after school and during school holidays, Mr. Atkinson worked first in the stockroom and then on the sales floor, earning money for his further education. Now he's been hired by Ernesta Costa to give the store a new look. Ms. Costa, who happens to be store founder Lloyd Robbin's granddaughter, says the store is doing well with business from both residents and tourists, but she feels it needs updating. "I interviewed several designers and was particularly impressed with Fred's ideas. The fact that he already had a deep knowledge of the store was a definite plus," said Ms. Costa.

Mr. Atkinson's concept will preserve many of the classic touches of the old store. For example, the beautiful carved doorway and marble stairway at the main entrance will not be replaced. On the other hand, the showrooms will be redecorated, and the fitting rooms will be upgraded. The store will remain open during the process, and a grand reopening event is scheduled for the second week of October.

161. What is the purpose of the article?
(A) To advertise employment opportunities.
(B) To offer a profile of a new entrepreneur.
(C) To announce renovations to a business.
(D) To comment on tourism industry trends.

162. Who most likely is Mr. Atkinson?
(A) A university student.
(B) A tour leader.
(C) A store owner.
(D) An interior designer.

163. The word "touches" in paragraph 3, line 2, is closest, in meaning to
(A) modifications.
(B) features.
(C) contacts.
(D) sensations.

*GO ON TO THE NEXT PAGE.*

27

**Questions 164-167** refer to the following e-mail.

| To: | mora.simmons@heltlx.edu |
| From: | e.agbayani@periodicalquest.com |
| Date: | February 28 |
| Subject: | Periodical Quest |

Dear Ms. Simmons,

This is a courtesy message to inform you that your monthly Periodical Quest membership fee for March could not be processed due to an expired credit card. To avoid any service disruptions, please visit periodicalquest.com/useraccount and update your billing information. If you have any difficulties, I will be happy to take you through the process. Incidentally, while reviewing your account I noticed that you are not using our full range of services. As a member, you have unlimited online access to our library of over 3,000 journals, newspapers, and magazines. Additionally, as a professor you can also benefit from our resources for teaching and research purposes. It would seem that you did not complete your member profile when you signed up for our service four months ago. Please take a moment to review your member preferences. We want to make sure that you are taking advantage of all that Periodical Quest has to offer.

Feel free to contact me if you have any questions regarding your account. If you wish to cancel your membership, no further action is required.

Sincerely,

Elesa Agbayani
Periodical Quest

---

**164.** Why was Ms. Simmons contacted?
(A) A new service is now available.
(B) A payment was not processed.
(C) An order will be delivered soon.
(D) An article needs to be revised.

**165.** What is indicated about Periodical Quest?
(A) It charges a monthly fee.
(B) It has just doubled its journal collection.
(C) Its website is easy to navigate.
(D) Its customer support team is available 24 hours a day.

**166.** Who most likely is Ms. Agbayani?
(A) A magazine editor.
(B) A bank representative.
(C) A computer programmer.
(D) An accounts manager.

**167.** What is suggested about Ms. Simmons?
(A) She works in the field of education.
(B) She wants to cancel her membership.
(C) She has been traveling overseas.
(D) She has missed a deadline.

## Chad Wallace Helps Toronto Go Green

By Steve Lee

TORONTO (May 8)—Members of the Green Toronto Society have announced the winners of this year's Eco Awards to be presented at the annual Eco-Honors Banquet in July. This year's business prize will go to Toronto's very own environmentalist and entrepreneur Chad Wallace for his work in sustainable hospitality. Mr. Wallace opened the Wallace Inn in downtown Toronto just last year. — [1] — Its 50 guest rooms offer all the comforts of traditional accommodation but with minimal environmental impact. Solar panels, energy-efficient lighting, and smart indoor-climate control keep the building's energy use low. — [2] —

Anton Wong, head of the Green Toronto committee, noted that Mr. Wallace was selected for the prize not only for making his business sustainable, but also for sponsoring cleanup days at Toronto's parks. He has even purchased eco-friendly sculptures for placement throughout the city as part of a municipal sustainability awareness initiative. — [3] — "Mr. Wallace recognizes that increasing awareness of environmental issues is not possible through regulations alone. We need to engage the community as well," Mr. Wong said. "Although he has lived here for only a year, we feel that he represents many of the goals that the Green Toronto Society is working toward." — [4] —

**168.** According to the article, what will take place in July?
(A) A grand opening.
(B) An art exhibition.
(C) A celebration dinner.
(D) A park cleanup.

**169.** What type of business does Mr. Wallace run?
(A) A restaurant.
(B) A hotel.
(C) An engineering firm.
(D) A construction company.

**170.** What is indicated about Mr. Wallace?
(A) He supports community projects.
(B) He sculpts as a hobby.
(C) He holds a political office.
(D) He has a background in engineering.

**171.** In which of the positions marked [1], [2], [3], and [4] does the following sentence best belong?
"Even the property's decor consists of mostly recycled materials."
(A) [1].
(B) [2].
(C) [3].
(D) [4].

GO ON TO THE NEXT PAGE.

**Questions 172-175** refer to the following text-message chain.

*✗acoustic*
*adj. 聽覺的, 音響的*

| |
|---|
| **Rosa Gonzalez [10:02 A.M.]** Hi, Anna. Ken and I are at the conference hotel. Where are you? 我們在飯店了. 你在哪裡? 有會議室的飯店 |
| **Anna Losch [10:05 A.M.]** Waiting for a taxi at the airport. The traffic is horrible. It'll probably take me at least an hour to get to the hotel. 交通狀況非常糟. 勁要一小時才能到飯店 |
| **Rosa Gonzalez [10:06 A.M.]** We ran into the same thing yesterday. I think there's road construction in the area. 我們昨天也遇到同樣的事. 我想那區有在做路 |
| **Anna Losch [10:08 A.M.]** Do you know when Vijay Rau is speaking? I'd like to attend his session on acoustic designs for office buildings. 我想參加他的關於辦公大樓聽覺設計的課程(隔音設計) 可以幫我寫筆記嗎? |
| **Ken Yamamoto [10:09 A.M.]** At 11:00 this morning. 我到不了 |
| **Anna Losch [10:10 A.M.]** //I won't make it.// Can one of you take notes for me? 我也沒期待飛 Mr. Rau 要說什麼 |
| **Rosa Gonzalez [10:11 A.M.]** I'm looking forward to hearing what Mr. Rau has to say, too. One of the offices I'm designing requires acoustic tiles. 其中一間我設計的辦公室要我吸音磚. 事實上所有課程都有錄音 |
| **Ken Yamamoto [10:13 A.M.]** Actually, all sessions are getting recorded. You can watch his talk on the conference website later. 你晚點可以在會議網上看他的演講 |
| **Anna Losch [10:14 A.M.]** OK. I'll text you both after. I'll check in and drop off my luggage in my room. 我晚點會傳訊息給你們. 我會先辦理入住然後放行李 |
| **Rosa Gonzalez [10:16 A.M.]** I made reservations for us to have lunch in the lobby restaurant at noon. 我幫大家預約中午在大廳餐廳午餐 |
| **Anna Losch [10:17 A.M.]** Good, but it's going to be a working meal. We need to go over the slides for our design presentation so we have time to make any revisions. 但這會是工作午餐. 我們要把展示的幻燈片(PPT)看一次, 這樣我們才會有時間修訂 |

*revise v. 修正, 修訂*

**172.** Where do the people most likely work?
B
(A) At an airport. 建築公司 architect
(B) At an architectural firm. 建築師
(C) At a recording studio. 錄音室
(D) At an event-planning company. 策劃公司

**173.** At 10:10 A.M., what does Ms. Losch
D most likely mean when she writes, //"I won't make it."//? 班機晚到
(A) Her flight arrived late. 沒有預約房間
(B) She did not reserve a room.
(C) Her presentation is not ready. 展示是沒準備好
(D) She will miss a session. 會錯過一堂課

(A)要先註冊 (B)被重新排程 (C)線上很快
**174.** What does Mr. Yamamoto indicate 可以
C about Mr. Rau's session? 看到
(A) It required advance registration.
(B) It is being rescheduled.
(C) It will soon be available online.
(D) It will be held in an auditorium.
↳會在禮堂舉辦

**175.** What will the group most likely do at
A noon? 審查一場展示(報告)
(A) Review a presentation. 參加特殊
(B) Attend a special session. 活動
(C) Interview Mr. Rau. 面試
(D) Check into a hotel. 訪談 Mr.Rau

# Make Rock Star DJ the host of your next special event!

Rock Star DJ has been providing personalized musical entertainment services since 1999. While best known for its wedding DJ services, the company provides exceptional entertainment for teen dance parties, family celebrations, corporate events, bar and bat mitzvahs, music video parties, bar/club karaoke and trivia challenges.

**WEDDING PACKAGES**

All of our Wedding Packages offer an in-person planning meeting for that personalized touch. Choose from five packages (Ambience, Radiance, Brilliance, Vision, Concierge) and an exciting array of options. To see these packages and upgrades in action, please check out the videos on our website at https://wStardj.com./weddings

For those couples who appreciate the finer things in life, be sure to read about our recently launched "Concierge Package" that features live musicians and an incredible array of upgrades.

### Add a Photo Booth to any package for just $899!

| From: | Ned Rockland <nedrocks@rockstardj.com> |
|---|---|
| To: | Lorenzo Summers <losum@omail.org> |
| Re: | Your Wedding Package |
| Date: | June 12 |

Dear Mr. Summers,

謝謝對你付款購買幻象方案+拍照亭. 感謝你的購買. 可以參與你女兒11/17的

Thank you for your payment of $3,389 for the Vision package plus Photo Booth.

We appreciate your business, and it was <u>an honor</u> to be a part of your  婚禮是我們的

daughter's wedding on November 17.  The <u>video montage</u> has just returned  榮幸

from the editing studio, which you can download it at:  影片剪輯片段剛從剪輯公司

https:www.rockstardj.com/summers-frankel-wedding  送回來,你可以從這裡下載

還有,你的DVD複本會盡快寄送給你

In addition, your DVD copy will be sent ASAP.

你有提到你想訂所有的數位照片

You mentioned that you wanted to order digital copies of all pictures taken in

the Photo Booth.  We offer three options for Photo Booth Archiving.

我們提供3種選擇關於 "照片亭檔案" archive

**Price List:**                                                                                  n. 檔案

16 MB USB card — $99.99

32 MB USB flash drive — $139.99

784 MB Green-Ray DVD — $249.00

至於你公司9月會議中提供娛樂的事                               我很抱歉的說

<u>As for</u> providing entertainment at your corporate meeting in September, I regret

to say that we will be <u>unable</u> to <u>accommodate</u> you as we are completely booked

through October.  However, I'd be happy to refer you to an associated company

who may be available on short notice.  Let me know and I'll forward you her

contact information.

我們將無法西己合你,因為我們到10月都完全訂滿了

但是,我很樂意介紹你去相關的公司,可能短時間內通知

也有空的公司. 讓我知道. 若你需要我會把她的聯絡資訊

Sincerely,                                                                                     給你

Ned Rockland

Proprietor, Rock Star DJ and Entertainment Services, Inc.

\* on short notice   \* accommodate

一接到通知        v. 能容納. 使適應. 向~提供. 通融

The bank will accommodate him with a loan. 借他貸款

The hotel can accommodate 500 tourists.

**176.** According to the advertisement, what can be added to any package for $899? 根據廣告,什麼可以用899元加購

(A) A fog machine. 噴霧器
(B) A photo booth. → 照片亭
(C) A large video screen. 大的螢幕
(D) A live band. 現場演奏樂團

B

**177.** What is NOT mentioned in the advertisement as an event serviced by Rock Star DJ? 哪一個不是

(A) Bar mitzvahs.
(B) Funerals. 喪禮
(C) Corporate events.
(D) Trivia challenges.

B

Rock Star DJ
廣告中有提到的服務項目呢?

**178.** What is indicated about the wedding that took place on November 17? 關於11/9的婚禮何者敘述為真?

(A) It took place at Summers's corporate headquarters. 在公司總部舉行
(B) It featured a karaoke competition. 有卡啦OK比賽
(C) It was <u>coordinated</u> by Mr. Summers. 由Mr. Summers 主導.
(D) It was captured on video. 有用影片拍攝紀錄下來

D

**179.** What is included in the e-mail?

(A) Results of a customer survey.
(B) Descriptions of wedding packages.
(C) A practice schedule.
(D) A price list.

D

**180.** What does the <u>associated</u> company mentioned in the e-mail probably specialize in?

(A) Teaching music to children.
(B) Catering corporate events.
(C) Musical entertainment.
(D) Editing photographs.

C

* coordinate
v. 協調. 調節
→ If we coordinate our efforts we should be able to win the game.
如果我們同心協力.
應該能打勝這場比賽.

179.
(A) 客戶調查的結果
(B) 婚禮套裝的描述
(C) practice
n. 實施. 練習. 學習. 習慣. 常規. 慣例
(D) 價格清單

＊associated
adj. 聯合的. 關聯的

＊associate
n. 夥伴. 同事. 合夥人
adj. 合夥的. 夥伴的
副的
He is an associate editor of the newspaper.

180.
信裡提到的同業公司可能專業是什麼?
(A) 教小孩音樂
(B) 幫公司活動外燴
(C) 音樂娛樂
(D) 編輯照片

GO ON TO THE NEXT PAGE.

| From: | Luis Velarde |
|---|---|
| To: | Lily McVicker; Mercedes Watson; Doug Bo; Eric Hochhalter |
| Re: | Location Scouting ~scout 偵察.物色,嘲弄.不信~ |
| Date: | June 24 |

*181*
Most scientists scouted the new ~theory~.

📧 Locations – 24kb (Attachment: Word Doc)   *productive*

*=girls*   adj. 多產的. 有成效的. 肥沃的

Hey Guys and Gals!

我們昨天在 PC的商務午餐成效非常好.
I thought we had a very productive business lunch at Pedro's Cantina
身為 FR餐廳美國的最新成員, 天很高「成為Austin新分公司的
yesterday. As the newest member of the Fiesta Restaurant Group, I
團隊一員
am grateful to be part of the team that's opening the new franchising
在我們的會議當中   我無法不注意到)   (新分店)
office in Austin. During our meeting, I couldn't help but notice our
shared eagerness to expand FRG's business interests throughout the
state of Texas. 我們要把 FRG的生意拓展到整個德州的共同海望. (共同目標)
我有聽取你的建議關於新分店,的理想地點和位置
I've listened to your suggestions and concerns about our ideal space
and location for the new branch. Attached is a list and detailed
description of spaces from www.haydenrealty.com that meet our basic
criteria and budget. It's basically the best of the best; a short list of
    所
possibilities for everyone to look over. Please get back to me with
your feedback and comments.

Luis Velarde, Fiesta Restaurant Group

隨函附件是一張各單和詳細的地點
描述, 符合我們的基本判斷要求和預算

基本上是好中之好, 有個短的清單給大家看看
請回覆我你的想法和意見

ideal adj. 理想的, 完美的        idol n. 偶象
    + humidity               /aɪdl/
    + temperature
                          criterion (單) → criteria (複)
idea   n. 想法. 點子            判斷的標準/尺度
idea hamster 點子王

**4800 Landmark Blvd. Suite 500 — $2,000 (Travis Heights)**

繁華=熱鬧的區域

充滿前景的

開放式概念設計的辦公室,零售空間.位在流行的Travis Heights.附近是有前途的

Open concept office/retail space in trendy Travis Heights; up and coming

區域          有很多人行動

neighborhood with great foot traffic.  Super "green" building; eco-friendly

design will save you $$$ in energy costs.  Building has underground

parking.  Suite includes four reserved spaces. 超級綠色建築.環境友善設計

reserved

①.預約的②留作專用的③謹慎的            可以幫你省下能源開銷.大樓有地下室停車場

**124 Red River Street — $1,900 (Hancock)**    套房包含四個保留空間(預留空間)

↳She is very reserved.                        ✓有大門保全系統

Elegant first-floor 1,000-sq. meter office suite with gated security

  吡鄰的  Located at Hancock Center, adjacent to St. Paul's Hospital.  Just steps

/ə'dʒesənt/

from subway station and three stops from downtown.  Many high-profile

tenants.  Color copier/scanner/printer/fax on-site. 很多身分高檔的住戶

現場

**67 E. Cesar Chavez Street — $1,025 (Convention Center)**

獨立的.無需支撐的    多區域的          之前是汽車服務大樓

Free standing, multi-zoned.  Former automotive service building.  Can

   可以依據你的需求客製化          高級區. 正前方有高速公路183号

be customized to your requirements.  High area traffic with Highway 183

正前方      房東可以租可以賣

frontage.  Owner will lease or sell.  The building is on 0.3 acres.  Lot 一塊地

                                                              /eker/

next door of 0.3 acres is also for sale.  Located six blocks southeast of

the Convention Center.        位在東南方6個街區        1英畝=1224.12坪

                           的地方 ↳會議中心   0.3 ≒ 367.251坪

**5775 Airport Blvd #400 — $2,000 (North Loop)**

  4層樓辦公室      和市停車場吡鄰.每月有給住戶折扣通行證

Fourth-floor offices.  Adjacent city parking lot with discounted monthly

                    大樓有安全通過控制

permits for tenants.  Building has security access controls.  Located at

                        現代化的                      視訊會議

ACC Highland Industrial Park.  State-of-the-art Coldarrow video

conferencing; 4G high-speed wireless Internet included.

      4G高速無線網路也包含在內

*GO ON TO THE NEXT PAGE.* ➡

| From: | Eric Hochhalter |
|---|---|
| To: | Lily McVicker; Luis Velarde; Mercedes Watson; Doug Bo |
| Re: | Office Space |
| Date: | June 25 |

Dear Teammates,

First of all, kudos to Luis for taking the initiative and narrowing down our search to these options. It sounds like you guys made some major headway at the last minute. Sorry I missed it, but the situation at Pollo Paradise in Waco couldn't be helped. Since I'm the last to comment on this e-mail discussion, please be patient with me.

Mercedes, I appreciate your comments about being in a high-profile location with good transportation, but we can't lose sight of our priority, which is customizing a space to our specific needs. Is anyone familiar with public transportation in Austin? It would help to know if the building near the convention center has adequate public transportation.

I also agree with Luis's idea that we should make some inquiries down at the Austin Planning Commission about construction permits. (I will try to look into it this weekend when my wife and I attend the Austin Music Festival with my cousin, Roger, who attended University of Texas and is very familiar with real estate in the area.

Eric, FRG

**181.** Why did Mr. Velarde send the e-mail?
(A) To follow up on a meeting.
(B) To confirm a reservation at Pedro's Cantina.
(C) To organize a business trip.
(D) To inquire about some real estate.

**182.** What is one property feature mentioned in the attachment?
(A) A loading dock.
(B) A popular restaurant in the building.
(C) A video conferencing system.
(D) A nearby recreation center.

**183.** Which property does Mr. Hochhalter most likely favor?
(A) 4800 Landmark Boulevard.
(B) 124 Red River Street.
(C) 5775 Airport Boulevard.
(D) 67 E. Cesar Chavez Street.

**184.** What is indicated about Ms. Watson?
(A) She just moved to Hancock.
(B) She is the newest member of the team.
(C) She sent an e-mail to her colleagues.
(D) She used to live in North Loop.

**185.** What is suggested about Mr. Hochhalter?
(A) He missed the meeting at Pollo Paradise.
(B) He is considering a divorce.
(C) He plans to attend a performance.
(D) He went to college in Austin.

Questions 186-190 refer to the following letter and survey.

*indicate
v. 指出, 指示

His hesitation indicates unwillingness.
他的猶豫表明不願意
Please indicate to the organizers where you would like to sit.
請像主辦方表示, 說明自你想坐在何處

Home Works

June 24

Mr. Richard Metzer

2390 N. Clark Street

Chicago, IL 60625

感謝您成為 Home Works 的忠實顧客          我們的紀錄指出
Thank you for being a loyal Home Works customer. Our records indicate
你最近用聯名信用卡購買了東西
that you recently made a purchase with your Home Works Advantage 187
現在,          我們要執行一個簡單的調查關於你在 HW 的
credit card. At the moment, we are conducting a brief survey about your 186
購物經驗          隨函附件的調查應該不會花你
Home Works shopping experience. The enclosed survey should take no
超過 5分鐘來完成          而且我們要深深的感覺你的回覆 189
more than five minutes to complete and we would deeply appreciate your
一個已經付過錢, 回郵信封          已附在內以便你
feedback. A prepaid, self-addressed envelope is included for your
作為對你回覆的獎勵, 在7月3號前回覆的顧客
convenience. And as a reward for your patronage, customers who respond
會收到一整組 Ambrosia 香味蠟燭
before July 3 will receive a complete set of Ambrosia scented candles. 188

在7/3之後回覆的客人會收到一張
Those who return a completed survey after that date will receive a coupon
下次購物打9折的折價券
for 10 percent off of their next purchase.

先謝謝您的參加
Thank you in advance for your participation.

*patronage          *ambrosia
ɔ ɔ ɪ          |æmˊbroʒɪə|

Sincerely,          美味佳餚
Diana Williams          n. 贊助, 光臨          (神仙吃的美食)

Home Works Director of Customer Care
*participate          *scented 有香味的
v. 參加, 參與, 含有, 帶有

His poems participate of the nature of satire.
他的詩帶有諷刺的自然 (有諷刺意味)          +flowers
to participate in sth.          +sachet
          |sæˊʃe| 香袋

GO ON TO THE NEXT PAGE.
37

CUSTOMER SATISFACTION SURVEY 客戶滿意度調查

Customer name: Richard Metzger

Date: June 28

整體而言,你會如何評價你在 HW 的購物經驗?
Overall, how would you rate your shopping experience at Home Works?

| Not satisfied | | Satisfied | Very satisfied | |
|---|---|---|---|---|
| 1 | 2 | 3 | 4 | ⑤ |

你有幾分會想推薦 HW 給朋友呢?
How likely would you be to recommend Home Works to a friend?

| Not likely | | Somewhat likely | Very likely | |
|---|---|---|---|---|
| 1 | 2 | 3 | 4 | ⑤ |

你有在 HW 找到你所需要的東西嗎?
Did you find what you were looking for at Home Works?

| No | Yes |
|---|---|
| | (Yes) |

Which Home Works location did you visit? 你是去哪間店的?

Lincoln Avenue in Edgewater

Additional comments: 額外評論: 是我在芝加哥最喜歡的家飾用品店 員工超級友善
Home Works is my favorite <u>household furnishing store</u> in Chicago. The staff is extremely 有幫助
friendly and helpful, but I am most impressed by the incredible selection. I tell my friends
that if you can't find it at Home Works, you probably won't be able to find it.

Additional comments: ↙但是我對於他們超多的選擇,印象深刻
我跟朋友說,如果你在 HW 找不到的,你可能永遠不會找得到

---

**186.** Why did Ms. Williams write to Mr.
D Metzger? 宣布個人活動
(A) To announce a private event.
(B) To <u>deny</u> a refund. 拒絕一筆退款
(C) To confirm an order. 確認一筆訂單
(D) To <u>ask for</u> some feedback. 要求一些回饋

**187.** What is indicated about Home Works?
A (A) It issues credit cards to customers. (A) 有發信用卡給客戶
(B) It carries high-end merchandise. 賣高端商品
(C) It is opening a new location in Edgewater. 開新的店
(D) It is hiring sales staff. 在招募銷售員工

**188.** What will Mr. Metzger most likely
A receive from Home Works?
(A) A set of candles. 一組蠟燭
(B) A discount coupon. 優惠券
(C) A follow-up phone call. 跟進的電話
(D) An extra set of towels.

**189.** In the letter, the word "appreciate" in
A paragraph 1 line 5 is closest in meaning to
(A) be thankful for. 感恩
(B) authorize. 授權
(C) dismiss.
(D) disclose.

**190.** What does Mr. Metzger mention
D about Home Works?
(A) Its products are often out of stock. 商品常常缺貨
(B) Its sales people are not helpful. 銷售人員幫不上忙
(C) It has the lowest prices. 有最低的價格
(D) It has a wide variety of items. 有很廣的商品

夠的一組鐘

*compensation* 償還、賠償、津貼
→ The job is hard but the compensation is good.

教育補貼方案

# EDUCATION REIMBURSEMENT PROGRAM

again | into | purse

*permanent* adj. 永恆的、常在的、固定的

Argus Allied LLC's Education Reimbursement Program
協助全職員工,想得到更高專業知識或技巧的

assists permanent employees who want to attain higher
達到、獲得

levels of professional skills and knowledge. Educational
專業技巧和知識

教育的協助

assistance may cover up to 75 percent of the cost of tuition. 191
可能可以涵蓋至多75%的學費

It may also be used for the completion of approved
這筆補助也可以使用於完成和工作相關、有聯合、在任何受認可大學修的課程

job-related classes leading to a degree from any accredited 195

university. Course materials and other fees are not eligible
課程素材(教材)和其他費用不符合這筆補貼

for reimbursement.

*accredit* v. 委派、認可

*eligible* adj. 符合法律、符合資格的

Not all courses are automatically considered job-relevant.
並不是所有課程都自動被認為和工作相關

The Director of Human Resources will determine whether
人資部主管將決定這個課程和學分是否符合

a course or degree meets the guidelines of the Education
符合 方針 教育補貼方案的方針

Reimbursement Program. Employees must submit a
員工必須繳交一張課程同意表格

course approval form to the Human Resources Department 192
給人資部門,在註冊之前,才能得到補助的資格

before enrolling in a course in order to be eligible for

assistance.

* enroll { in / on / for } the course at the college.

* He enrolled as a part-time student.
They want to enroll their children in the local school.
想讓孩子註冊當地的學校

*GO ON TO THE NEXT PAGE.*

| From: | Edward Bloom <e_bloom@argus.com> |
| To: | Molly Zhang <m_zhang@argus.com> |
| Re: | Approval for courses |
| Date: | Molly Zhang <m_zhang@argus.com> |

✉ EAAF Approval Form – 13.9kb (Attachment: Word Doc)

Dear Mr. Bloom,

我打算下學期夜間課程在 Hempford 大學修 2 門課

I am planning to take two courses at Hempford University

during the upcoming semester in the evening program. At

照這樣的上法下去，我可以在明年12月以前完成復學碩士學位.

this rate, I should be finished with the Accelerated Master's

before

Degree program by December of next year. I have attached

我已隨函附件附上同意表格        其中一門課還有最後確定的日期

the approval form to this e-mail. One of the courses does

但我被告知，要在10月初開課

not have finalized dates yet, but I was **told** that it would start

in early October. As soon as I get your approval, I will

officially enroll in the courses online.

一旦我收到你的批准.

我會正式的線上報名

登記

Thank you, 報名參加          *course

入伍,入學          n.路線.方向

Molly Zhang          過程.科目.一道菜

方針.做法  I think the only sensible course

is to retreat.

---

* accelerate          我覺得唯一明智的做法是撤退

v. 使增速.促進.增加          v.流動  Tears coursed down her face.

The bad weather accelerated          她淚.流滿面

our departure.

糟糕的天氣使我們早日離開          * approve

The car suddenly accelerated.          v. 贊成.同意.批准.認可

汽車突然加快了速度          I am afraid that your parents won't approve

of your going there.

不會贊成你到那兒去

approval

n. 批准.認可.同意

## Educational Assistance Approval Form

*Employee Information*

Employee name : Molly Zhang 客服代表人員
Position : Customer Care Representative
Division : Customer Service

工作相關的課程資訊
*Work-related Class Information*

Degree sought : 機構名稱 Master of Business Administration
Name of institution : Hempford University
Name of course : 課程名程 International Finance　(A) 申請修課許可
Course starting date : September 14　　permission
Course ending date : December 9　　許可證, 許可. 允許

Name of course : Leadership Development　(B) 宣傳新的教育
Course starting date : To Be Determined　　課程
Course ending date : To Be Determined　(C) 要一封推薦信

(A) 讓員工在家上班　　(C) 付部分的學費　　(D) 建議一個政策的
(B) 允許有彈性的工作時間　(D) 負擔講義/教科書的錢　　改變

**191.** How does the company assist
employees with education?
(A) It lets employees work at home.
(B) It allows flexible work schedules.
(C) It pays for part of the tuition.
(D) It covers the cost of textbooks.

要徑人資部 approval, 所以 Bloom 是人資部

**192.** In what department does Mr. Bloom
most likely work? 永續教育
(A) Continuing Education.
(B) Product development. 商品開發
(C) Customer Service. 客服
(D) Human Resources. 人資

**193.** When will the leadership development
course most likely begin? ↓
(A) In June.　尚未決定開課日期的課
(B) In September.　可能10月初開課
(C) In October.
(D) In December.　#affiliate
v. 使併入. 使耕屬  n. 分支機構

**194.** What is the purpose of the e-mail?
(A) To apply for permission to take
classes.
(B) To promote a new educational
program. ≈a recommendation
(C) To ask for a letter of reference.
(D) To suggest a change to a policy.

要得到教育補助需要什麼?

**195.** What is required to obtain educational
assistance? 一定要是線上課程.
(A) The courses must be completed
online. 學分課程要和工作有關
(B) The degree program must be
relevant to the job.
(C) The university must be affiliated
with Juniper Allied. 一定要耕屬杜松
(D) The employee must attend classes
at night. 聯盟

一定要是夜間課程

(像長春藤系列一樣)

GO ON TO THE NEXT PAGE.

41

www.activeathletics.com

| Home | Products | Support | Vendors |

BPAA™
Quality Award
5-Star Rating

# ACTIVE ATHLETICS ONLINE

## THE #1 ON-LINE SPORTING GOODS RETAILER

Get pumped up!! with the best-selling

## Proflex 5.1 Utility Weight Bench

### THIS WEEK ONLY!!!!!

~~Unbeliev~~able Price!

Order today, use it tomorrow

$229.00 >>> $159.99*

includes taxes and overnight delivery

Take an extra $10 off with coupon code: ACTIVENOW

*"The Proflex 5.1 fully-adjustable weight bench is the industry standard in fitness centers across the U.S.!"*
— Tom Johnson, fitness expert

This week only, save 30% on Proflex, the hottest name in exercise equipment! Our warehouses are jammed to capacity, so we're slashing prices and clearing our inventory in order to make way for the next generation of exercise equipment.

42

| From: | Ace Derrick <ace_d@pueblo.com> |
|---|---|
| To: | Active Athletics <customerservice@activeathletics.com> |
| Re: | Order Reference #EH-28934 訂單編號 |
| Date: | August 16 |

這是我過去二週以來寄的第四封信了. 我尚未收到回應或是關於舉重椅的解釋.
This is the fourth e-mail I have sent in the past two weeks, and I have yet
我也打電話給
to receive a response or an explanation about the weight bench. I've also called
1-800 到10幾次, 只得到 等待 無限等待的回應 無期限地
the 1-800 number at least a dozen times, only to be put on hold indefinitely.
電話等待 (下)
如我提供佐證的電話號碼和確認郵件你寄的
As evidenced by both the reference number and the confirmation e-mail you
我8/1用折扣券在你們網上買了 Proflex 5.1
sent, I purchased the Proflex 5.1 from your website on August 1 using the

coupon code. The website clearly stated that (a) the bench was in stock, and

(b) it would be shipped overnight. 網站上明確的說 舉重椅有庫存
(下) 而且會隔日到貨.

This is hardly the kind of service I would expect from the "#1 Online Retailer".

However, I do expect one of the following two things to happen within the next
①                                    ②
48 hours. Either I receive the weight bench, or you refund my money. Keep in

mind that whatever happens, I intend to report Active Athlete to the Bureau of

Consumer Fraud.

這不太會是我預期從"第一名線上電售店"得到的服務
品而, 我還是期待接下來的48小時之內會發生
Please respond appropriately.                 其中一件事情.
請依合適的方式回覆
                                    要嘛. 我收到舉重椅. 或是你退我錢
Ace Derrick  (4者的解決辦法)  記住, 不管發生什麼, 我意欲 (想要) 舉報
                                    Active Athlete 給「消費者詐騙處」

# indefinitely
adv. 不定地. 無期限地. 不明確地
→ You can borrow the book indefinitely.
→ She expressed herself rather indefinitely. 她含糊地表達了自己的想法

* hardly
adv. 幾乎不. 簡直不:   我的腿虛弱的無法站立   My legs were so weak that I could hardly stand.
 (幾. 剛)           : He had hardly arrived when it began to snow.
        他一到. 天就下雪了

GO ON TO THE NEXT PAGE.

**196.** Why is the Proflex 5.1 Weight Bench on sale?

B

(A) The company facing expensive litigation. 訴訟.爭訟

(B) The company needs room for new products. 公司需要空間放新商品

(C) It has been replaced by a newer model. 被更新的型號取代了

(D) It has been recalled by the manufacturer. 已經被製造商召回

**197.** What does the advertisement NOT promise? 廣告沒有答應哪項?

B

(A) Online savings. 線上省錢

(B) Warranty. 保固

(C) Taxes included. 含稅

(D) Overnight delivery. 隔夜(隔日)到貨

**198.** In the advertisement, paragraph 1, line 4, what is the closest meaning of "inventory"?

B

(A) options 選擇

(B) stock 庫存

(C) storage 儲存

(D) utility

↓ ① 水電瓦斯

⊂ ② 效用·功利

The store deals in objects of domestic utility.

那家商店出售家庭用品

adj. 多用途的

a utility knife 多用途小刀

**199.** How much did Ace Derrick most likely pay for the bench?

C

(A) $99.99.

(B) $139.99.

(C) $149.99.

(D) $229.99 plus tax and delivery.

**200.** What did Ace Derrick ask the company to do? 馬上聯絡他 (下)

A

(A) Contact him promptly.

(B) Send a different model. 寄不一樣的型號

(C) Give him store credit. 給他購物金

(D) File a complaint with the bureau.

向局處提出客訴(抗告) /bjʊrol/

局.事務處

* prompt

adj. 敏捷的.即時的.迅速的

He is prompt in paying his rent.

adv. 準時地

They started at 7:00 prompt.

→ *貯存.(知識的)積蓄

The sailor has a rich stock of tales of adventure.

水手滿肚子都是探險的故事

存貨.庫存品

There is not much stock in the shop right now.

目前店裡庫存不多.

v. 庫存 We stock all types of our coats.

我們有各種度衣供應

adj. 庫存的

慣用的.平凡的. I am tired of his stock reply.

我已經聽厭了他老一套的回答.

Stop! This is the end of the test. If you finish before time is called, you may go back to Parts 5, 6, and 7 and check your work.

# New TOEIC Speaking Test

## Question 1: Read a Text Aloud

 **Question 1**

**Directions:** In this part of the test, you will read aloud the text on the screen. You will have 45 seconds to prepare. Then you will have 45 seconds to read the text aloud.

*Zapmeto 董事會議預訂 4/2 (五) 早上 9:00 在總部舉辦*
A meeting of the Zapmeto Board of Directors has been scheduled

*head office*
for 9:00 A.M. on Friday, April 2, at our <u>headquarters</u>. You may join us

*你可以線上參與會議，若你無法親自參加。*     *行程表上的第一件事*
online if you are <u>unable</u> to <u>attend</u> in person. The first item on the

*不能的、不會的、無能力的、不能勝任的 = incapable = incompetent*
*= unqualified*
agenda will be to approve the list of planned <u>expenditures</u> for the

*即是同意(通過)，即將列來月份的消費支出計畫表 (上)*
upcoming month. As most of these are routine, the vote can be held   *可以一聚桌*

*這些大部分是固定行程 /ru'tin/ 日常工作，慣例*     *就開始投票*
immediately upon gathering. Following this vote, we will take an

*投票之後，我們會更深入看看，把幾個*
in-depth look at a <u>proposal</u> to move the <u>assembly lines</u> for several

*Zapmeto 商品組裝線搬移到 Lexington 工廠的計畫 (提案)*
Zapmeto products to the Lexington <u>plant</u>.

*＊assemble*      *n. ①. 植物   v. 栽種*
*v. 集合，召集，組裝*     *②工廠*
→ *He was busy assembling the bike.*     *＊ proposal*
     *n. 提議、求婚*
→ *The visiting parents assembled in the school hall.*     → *She has had a proposal.*
     *已經空有人向她求婚了*

| PREPARATION TIME |
|---|
| 00 : 00 : 45 |

| RESPONSE TIME |
|---|
| 00 : 00 : 45 |

*GO ON TO THE NEXT PAGE.*

# Question 2: Read a Text Aloud

*rapid*

It's a rapidly changing world.

growing economy.

🎧 5 🎧 **Question 2**

**Directions:** In this part of the test, you will read aloud the text on the screen. You will have 45 seconds to prepare. Then you will have 45 seconds to read the text aloud.

不管怎樣你都應該打電話請病假，因為你感冒了

Whether or not you should call in sick because you have a cold

視嚴重度不同 (視嚴重度而定)　adv.很快地，迅速地　如果你很快的清空

depends on its severity. If you are rapidly emptying boxes of tissues

面紙盒，並且有無法控制的咳　*你就是重感冒

and have an uncontrollable cough, you've got a pretty bad cold. You

你會沒辦法專心，還有可能散播細菌給別人

will have trouble concentrating and will likely spread germs to others.

如果你的感冒沒有那麼嚴重，而且你必須去工作，常洗手

If your cold is not that severe and you must go to work, wash your

並且保持你的電話和電腦無菌的狀態

hands frequently and keep your phone and computer germ-free by

若別人使用了，用酒精棉擦一擦

wiping them down with alcohol wipes if others use them. If your

酒精棉片

co-workers keep their distance, don't be offended. It may not be the

如果你的同事和你保持距離，不要覺得被冒犯

garlic dill you had with lunch, but instead their fear of catching what

可能不是因為你中午的大蒜醃製酸黃瓜

you have.　而是他們害怕染上你現在有的(病毒)

*wipe down　　*wipe v.擦　Wipe the table
擦乾淨　　　　　　　擦去 The paint won't wipe off easily.

| PREPARATION TIME |
| --- |
| 00 : 00 : 45 |

| RESPONSE TIME |
| --- |
| 00 : 00 : 45 |

70

# Question 3: Describe a Picture

 **Question 3**

**Directions:** In this part of the test, you will describe the picture on your screen in as much detail as you can. You will have 30 seconds to prepare your response. Then you will have 45 seconds to speak about the picture.

| PREPARATION TIME |
| --- |
| 00 : 00 : 30 |

| RESPONSE TIME |
| --- |
| 00 : 00 : 45 |

*GO ON TO THE NEXT PAGE.*

# Question 3: Describe a Picture

*load

v. 裝載.裝入 →Don't forget to load your camera.　n. 車掭.車任

大量給予 → His brothers and　**答題範例**　→ The good news has taken
sisters loaded him with books.　　　a load off my mind.

一車或一船的貨物

((6)) **Question 3**

→ The truck was carrying a
load of sand.

This is a picture of some people in the parking lot of a department
store. 這張圖是有些人在百貨公司的停車場裡頭

There are three men and one woman. 有3男一女

The woman is pushing a <u>shopping cart</u>. 女的在推購物車

購物車裡有幾個購物袋
The shopping cart <u>contains</u> a couple of shopping bags.

The woman has just purchased some things. 女生剛買了些東西

She seems <u>pleased with herself</u>. 她看起來對自己很滿意

右邊兩個男生穿T-shirt
The two men on the right are wearing T-shirts.

The man on the left is wearing a polo shirt. 左邊的男生穿polo衫

Two of them have the same logo on their shirts.
其中有兩個人衣服上有一樣的標誌

這些男生很可能是百貨的員工
The men are most likely employees of the department store.

They are accompanying the woman to her car. 他們陪這個女生去車上

They will probably help the woman <u>load</u> her <u>purchases</u> into her car.

可能會幫助這位女士把她購買的東西裝上車

The man on the left looks like a manager type. 左邊的男人看起來像經理

He's wearing long pants, too. 他也穿著長褲

The other two look like they're still in college. 另外兩位看起來

我看到背景有一些人　　　　　仍舊在念大學
I see a couple of people in the background.

I can see the entrance to the department store. 可以看到百貨的入口

There's at least one other car in the parking lot.
至少有一台其他車在停車場

72

# Questions 4-6: Respond to Questions

 **Question 4**

**Directions:** In this part of the test, you will answer three questions. For each question, begin responding immediately after you hear a beep. No preparation time is provided. You will have 15 seconds to respond to Questions 4 and 5 and 30 seconds to respond to Question 6.

Imagine that a U.S. marketing firm is doing research in your country. You have agreed to participate in a telephone interview about shopping malls.

## Question 4

The last time you visited a shopping mall, how much time did you spend in the mall?

## Question 5

When you make a purchase at a shopping mall, what do you usually buy?

## Question 6

Describe one service or policy at your favorite shopping mall that you would like to change.

GO ON TO THE NEXT PAGE.

# Questions 4-6: Respond to Questions

*買東西會遇到的句子*

答題範例　Q: May I help you?
Are you looking for anything
in particular?

((6)) **Question 4**

A: I'm just browsing.
Yes, I am looking for a ＿＿＿

The last time you visited a shopping mall, how much time did you spend in the mall? 你上次去賣場的時候,你花多少時間在裡頭?

Q: Is this on sale?

**Answer**

A: It's 10% off
It's three for two.

我大概一週前去賣場
I visited the mall about a week ago.

The Galleria on La Brea Avenue.

I spent about an hour in the mall. 我大概花一小時在賣場裡

*Can you do me a deal? 可以給我折扣嗎?
Can you throw in any extras? 可以給一些贈品嗎?
Great, I'll take it!
Can you gift-wrap that? 可以幫我包裝嗎

((6)) **Question 5**

How would you like to pay?
Can I redeem this? ＜ gift card
discount voucher

When you make a purchase at a shopping mall, what do you usually buy?

你在賣場買東西的時候、你通常會買什麼?

**Answer**

我大部分買衣服
I mostly buy clothing.

有時候我買飾品
Sometimes I buy accessories.

我有時在美食街用餐
And I eat in the food court sometimes.

# Questions 4-6: Respond to Questions

## 🎧 6 Question 6

Describe one service or policy at your favorite shopping mall that you would like to change. 請描述一個服務或政策在你最喜歡商場裡你想改變的

## Answer

我希望可以有個私人的客戶休息室
I wish there was a private customer lounge.
我在一些高端的商場裡有看到過
I've seen them in other high-end malls.
他們就像是機場的常飛客俱樂部(休息室)
They're like the frequent flyer clubs at the airport.

休息室有乾淨的廁所和可以坐的地方
The lounge has clean restrooms and places to sit.
有地方可以哺乳並且換尿布          /名詞/
There's a place for <u>breastfeeding</u> and changing <u>diapers.</u>
他們有小小的吧台，可以買飲料
They have a little bar where you can buy a drink.

                                                    ≠ access
                                              n. 接近入口
你付會員費進入
You pay a membership fee for |access.|        病的發作，病的爆發
可以休息一下                                  in an access of hurry
It's good for taking a break.
我知道有很多人花很多時間在商場裡        勃然大怒
I know a lot of people who spend hours at the mall.

*GO ON TO THE NEXT PAGE.*

 Question 7

**Directions:** In this part of the test, you will answer three questions based on the information provided. You will have 30 seconds to read the information before the questions begin. For each question, begin responding immediately after you hear a beep. No additional preparation time is provided. You will have 15 seconds to respond to Questions 7 and 8 and 30 seconds to respond to Question 9.

什麼是認可的老師訓練
一是個教育的課程.要所在加州可以
也可以補充教學準備"
包含有人監督的教學,通常稱為
被說知修.試教.學生教學

有哪些教學證照?
早教.藝術.特教.心理.
學.不同課需要不同的證
照

教師證.主要要求是什麼?
各州有自己的標準.但大部分需要
* 區域認證學校的大學文憑
* 州的教師考試成績
* 完成"認可的老師訓練活動"

→所有的老師都需要有證照嗎?
有些州.代課老師不同證照
說多私校老師不用教學證
但是所有公學校老師都要
有還他們要任教州的教學證

什麼是初始或臨時的教師證
→這張免費時的證.發給許多新老師
6老師就算沒通過"要認可老師訓練"
也可以在有限的時間內在學校系統內
像了果.高次要的標準符合後
他們可以成為專業的有證教師

什麼是專業或標準教師證
這個證是給老師已用初始/臨時
證教張多年的人
在得到專業之證之前
老師要有完成任一項傑出的
要求.如:通過標準考試的成績

Hi, I'm interested in the teacher certification. Would you mind if I asked a few questions?

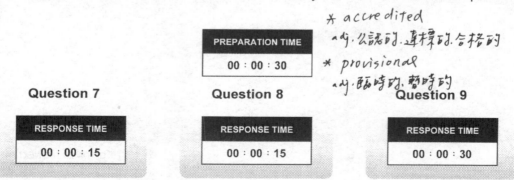

* accredited
→ 少. 公認的. 達標的. 合格的
* provisional
→ 少. 臨時的. 暫時的

| PREPARATION TIME |
| --- |
| 00 : 00 : 30 |

| Question 7 | Question 8 | Question 9 |
| --- | --- | --- |
| RESPONSE TIME | RESPONSE TIME | RESPONSE TIME |
| 00 : 00 : 15 | 00 : 00 : 15 | 00 : 00 : 30 |

# Questions 7-9: Respond to Questions Using Information Provided

答題範例

\* certificate

(n)證明書、證券.

a degree certificate

學位證書

(v) 發證書、用證書證明

**((6))** **Question 7**

What are the main requirements for teacher certification?

教師證的主要要求是什麼?

Her good character is certified.

**Answer**

區域認可學校的大學文憑.

*1* A bachelor's degree from a regionally accredited school.

國內老師考試的通過分數

*2* A passing score on a state teacher exam.

完成一個認可的老師訓練課程

*3* Completion of an approved teacher training program.

\* certify

證明: The witnesses must certify that this is your signature.

擔保: certify a check

**((6))** **Question 8**

所有的老師都需要有證照嗎?

Do all teachers need to be certified?

發證照: certify a teacher

**Answer**

在某些州.代課老師和老師小助手不需要證照

In some states, substitute teachers and teacher aides do

助手

not need to be certified.

大部分的私校老師沒有被要求持有教學證照

Most <u>private school</u> teachers are not required to hold a

teaching license.

但是.所有公立學校老師應該要有證照

However, all <u>public school</u> teachers must be certified.

*GO ON TO THE NEXT PAGE.*

((● 6 ●)) **Question 9**

臨時的.和標準的教師證差別在哪裡？

What is the difference between provisional and standard teaching certifications?

*He granted me my request.*
*Are you going to grnt that I was right?*

ⓥ
③同意
⑤承認
ⓓ授與.

**Answer**

The provisional certificate is a temporary license <u>granted</u>

to many new teachers.

讓老師們可以在州系統內工作
It allows a teacher to work in the state system.

只在有限的時間內有效.
It's only <u>valid for</u> a limited amount of time.

adj. 有根據的.令人信服的. *Her arguement is valid.*
合法的.有效的 *a valid contract*

Teachers on a provisional certificate have not completed

有臨時證的老師就是尚未完成訓練課程
the training course.

They may or may not have passed the exam.

It's assumed they will eventually earn a standard

teaching license. 假設他們最後會得到標準的教學證

★ earn 掙得. *How much do you earn a week?*

使得到 *His achievements earned him respect and*
The standard license is <u>earned</u> after several years of *admiration.*

得到尊敬和仰慕
teaching under a provisional license.

Additionally, all other requirements must be met.

I hope that answers your question.

# Question 10: Propose a Solution

 **Question 10**

**Directions:** In this part of the test, you will be presented with a problem and asked to propose a solution. You will have 30 seconds to prepare. Then you will have 60 seconds to speak. In your response, be sure to show that you recognize the problem, and propose a way of dealing with the problem.

In your response, be sure to

- show that you recognize the caller's problem, and
- propose a way of dealing with the problem.

PREPARATION TIME
00 : 00 : 30

RESPONSE TIME
00 : 01 : 00

GO ON TO THE NEXT PAGE.

# Question 10: Propose a Solution

## 答題範例

**Voice Message**

我是 AA農場的 Trisha，我們在貴公司下訂單、

1500個要送草莓的盒子

  Hello, this is Trisha from Ann Arbor Farms. We placed an

因為這周的壞天氣，我們比預計的早需要這些盒子

order with your company for 1,500 boxes for transporting

strawberries. Because of the bad weather this week, we're

眼下這個時候 (at this stage)

going to need the boxes earlier than expected. I'm sorry to

抱歉改變了草送日期     但我別無送擇

change the delivery date for our order at this stage, but I don't

我們將會損失這些草莓，如果我們無法儘快在

have a choice—we'll lose the strawberries if we can't box them

採收時將他們裝起來   我不想找別的供應商

as soon as they're harvested. I don't want to call a different

請讓我知道你是否能夠訂符合 (配合) 我們訂單的

supplier. Please let me know whether you'll be able to

新草送日期

accommodate the new delivery date for our order.

* at this stage

暫時 =
| temporary | for the moment |
| provisional | for the time being |
| impermanent | for a while |

眼下 =
| at the moment | right now |
| at present | for the time being |

# Question 10: Propose a Solution

## 答題範例

我收到你的訊息了

***Hi, Trisha, I got your message.***

I understand that you need the boxes sooner than originally requested. 我理解你比平常要求的更快需要盒子

I also recognize the urgency of your situation. 我也明白你現在情況 的緊急性

我們想盡力做來維持(保持)你的生意
We want to do everything we can to keep your business.

We don't want you to look for another supplier. 我們不希望你找別的 供應商

We will do whatever it takes.
我們會不計代價出貨.

壞天氣同時也妨礙了我們的貨運          * hamper 妨礙
                                              x
The bad weather has also hampered our deliveries.

我們實際上有好多筆訂單都遲了          ahead of schedule
We're actually behind schedule on a number of orders.          behind schedule

Everybody is feeling the squeeze. 每個人都感受到了齊壓

                                              (壓力)(困境)

同時,我有個想法
***Meanwhile, I have an idea.***

我今天先送一半的貨給你
I could ship half of your order today.
明天某個時間貨會到.
It would arrive sometime tomorrow.

然後,我會在這周結束前寄給你
And then, I could ship the other half <u>by the end of the week</u>.

You won't lose any strawberries. 你不會損失任何草莓

So, I think that would be <u>the best course of action</u>.          * course
                                                                      / kors/
所以,我想那是這個動作最好的解決方法
                                                                      n. 路線.方針.做法
Let me know if this works. 如果行行跟我說一下          深程.菜

Let me know if you have other questions.          v. 流動

Give me a call. 若你有任何其他問題          Tears coursed down her
                                              face.
跟我說一下
                                              淚從她臉上流下.

*GO ON TO THE NEXT PAGE.*

# Question 11: Express an Opinion

((• 5 •)) **Question 11**

**Directions:** In this part of the test, you will give your opinion about a specific topic. Be sure to say as much as you can in the time allowed. You will have 15 seconds to prepare. Then you will have 60 seconds to speak.

Some people crave routine in their daily lives while others thrive on change. What is your opinion about this? Give reasons for your opinion.

| PREPARATION TIME |
|:---:|
| 00 : 00 : 15 |

| RESPONSE TIME |
|:---:|
| 00 : 01 : 00 |

# Question 11: Express an Opinion

## 答題範例

 **Question 11**

嗯,我覺得每個人都有些不一樣
***Well, I think everybody is a little different.***

I know both types of people. 我兩種人都有認識.

I also know people who are a mix of both. 也有知道兩種個性混合的人

在生命的某些領域中,慣性.規律是更重要的
Routine is more important in some areas of life than others.

你想要公眾交通工具準時,每一次都準時
You want <u>public transportation</u> to run on time, every time.

But you don't want to eat the same thing for lunch every single day.
但是你不會想每一天午餐都吃一樣的東西

Routine can be a positive experience at work. 規律在工作上也可以是正向的經驗

Having the muscle memory of an activity makes it much easier to do.

You're <u>less likely</u> to make a mistake. 讓肌肉記憶某項活動.讓該活動更容易
執行
你比較不會出錯。 另一方面,我很容易覺得無聊
***On the other hand, I'm easily bored.***
我無法忍受一再重複做同樣的事
I can't stand doing the same thing over and over again.

I <u>need variety</u> in my daily tasks. 我每天的工作需要變化性

像"規律"一樣,"改變"的重要性也常不相同(變來變去)
Like routine, the importance of change varies.

你想盡可能的做新的事情
You want to see and do new things as often as possible.

But you don't want to quit a steady job <u>on a whim</u>. 但你又不想辭去穩定的工作因為
一時的念頭                一時的興起

Change is good <u>up until</u> it causes unexpected suffering.
直到改變引起無法預期的
Routine is positive as long as you're in control of what you're doing.
痛苦之前都是好事
Both have strengths and drawbacks. 規律是好的
2者都有優點和缺點. 又當你不能控制你在做的事

*GO ON TO THE NEXT PAGE.*

# New TOEIC Writing Test

## Questions 1-5: Write a Sentence Based on a Picture

### Question 1

**Directions:** Write ONE sentence based on the picture using the TWO words or phrases under it. You may change the forms of the words and you may use them in any order.

**attend / conference**

Many people attend the conference.

The conference is well attended.

答題範例：**Some people are attending a conference.**

*GO ON TO THE NEXT PAGE.*

# Questions 1-5: Write a Sentence Based on a Picture

## Question 2

**Directions:** Write ONE sentence based on the picture using the TWO words or phrases under it. You may change the forms of the words and you may use them in any order.

**witness / lawyer**

The witness made the lawyer angry.
The lawyer is standing right next to the witness.
The lawyer is looking the witness in the eye(s).
The witness is answering / responding (to) the lawyers questions.
         replying

答題範例：**The lawyer is** | **questioning the witness.**
           | asking the witness questions.

# Questions 1-5: Write a Sentence Based on a Picture

## Question 3

**Directions:** Write ONE sentence based on the picture using the TWO words or phrases under it. You may change the forms of the words and you may use them in any order.

**diver / board**

*diver
n. 潛水侠, 跳水者

* scuba-diving          preparing to do a back dive off the board.
  水肺潛水              standing very straight on the board.

* snorkelling 浮潛      using his arms to balance on the board.
                       standing at the edge of the board.

答題範例：**The diver is on the board.**

*GO ON TO THE NEXT PAGE.*

# Questions 1-5: Write a Sentence Based on a Picture

## Question 4

**Directions:** Write ONE sentence based on the picture using the TWO words or phrases under it.  You may change the forms of the words and you may use them in any order.

**pilot / cockpit**

答題範例：**Two pilots are in the cockpit.**

機艙

reviewing the checklist in the cockpit.
their checklists

A pilot in the cockpit is checking the (instrument) panel.

# Questions 1-5: Write a Sentence Based on a Picture

## Question 5

**Directions:** Write ONE sentence based on the picture using the TWO words or phrases under it. You may change the forms of the words and you may use them in any order.

**write / ticket**

答題範例：**The officer is writing a ticket.**

policeman                    traffic ticket

traffic cop

*GO ON TO THE NEXT PAGE.*

## Question 6

Directions: Read the e-mail below.

| | |
|---|---|
| **From:** c_lemm@encoremineral.com | |
| **To:** p_foster@kmail.com | |
| **Subject: Orientation Program** | |
| **Date: October 3** | |

Dear Mr. Foster,

你被邀參加 10/19 新員工 新訓、公司的政策和流程會包含在內. 還有

You are invited to attend the new employee <u>orientation program</u> on October 19. The company's <u>policies</u> and <u>procedures</u> will be covered as well as the services and benefits offered to employees. 提供給員工的服務及服利

請注意, 如你這樣的兼職員工也被要求參加.

Please note that part-time employees like you are also required to attend

這個活動將會在會議室舉行(是大樓的) 從早到下午1失

the meeting. The session will take place in the conference room of the Core Building and will run from 8 A.M. to 1 P.M. Lunch will be served afterward in the cafeteria of the Mantle Building. 會再供午餐, 在Mantle大樓的

之後      自助吧

在新訓開始之前, 請看員工手冊      因為那將是新訓活動

Before the orientation, please review the employee handbook that has been provided to you because it will <u>form the basis of the session</u>. 的基本主要貌

若你不克參加, 請通知分配給你部門的人資代表 LD

If you are unable to attend the meeting, please <u>notify</u> the Human Resources representative <u>assigned</u> to your department, Ms. Lauren DeBenedictus, as 要盡快 soon as possible. Ms. DeBenedictus can be reached (at) extension 3210 or at <u>p_debenedictus@emh.com</u>. 可以打分機 3210 或 e-mail

We look forward to seeing you.   *notify      *assign

Sincerely,
Carly Lemm
Assistant Director, Human Resources Department
Encore Mineral Holdings

新員工

以 Paul Foster 的身分寫給 DeBenedictus, 對於錯過新訓道歉並給一理由.

Directions: Write to Ms. DeBenedictus as Paul Foster, the new employee.
<u>Apologize for</u> missing the orientation program and give ONE reason why.

# Questions 6-7: Respond to a written request

## 答題範例

## Question 6

Dear Ms. DeBenedictus,

本來 10/19 我要參加員工新訓.  *be supposed to*

On October 19, I was supposed to attend the new employee orientation

然而(可是) 我前一晚覺得不舒服,我必須去看醫生

program.  However, I felt ill the night before, and I had to see a doctor.

我很喜 呈交醫生診單, 如果需要的話

I am happy to submit my doctor's note if needed.  Let me know if you

若你需要更多的細節,及其他我需要做到來滿足這個事的步驟    請告訴我。

require any further details and what other steps I should take to

adequately address this issue.  事件.期刊    (完成這段步驟)
充 分 工
通當地   對付,滿足
足夠地

Sincerely,

Paul Foster

# Questions 6-7: Respond to a written request

*analysis* n. ʒ æ ə ɪ      *analyst* n. 分析師 æ ɪ

## Question 7

*analyze* v. 分析 æ əɪ      *analyzer* n. 分解者 æ ə ɪ ɪ

Directions: Read the e-mail below.

| |
|---|
| From: Kenny Gould (k_gould@sharpmail.com) |
| To: Louise Minter (l_Minter@lauderdalefinancial.com) |
| Date: Thursday, July 18 |
| Subject: RE: Note from Kenny Gould |

Dear Ms. Minter,

謝謝你同意我的申請,讓我參加LF的股票分析師實習活動

Thank you for approving my application to join your internship program
(上) 實習生

as a stock analyst trainee at Lauderdale Financial. I very much look
我非常期等在你公司上班

forward to working at your firm, and I hope that I will be one of the
並且希望我特營成為高實習結束時
你們挑選作為全職員工的其中一名實習生

interns you select for a full-time position when the internship ends.

我唯一的考量是我目前報名3堂6周的密集珠程(不穩市場的準則)

My only concern is that I am currently enrolled in a six-week intensive
珠會上到7/29週五

course called Principles of Market Volatility, which runs until Friday,
a ɑ ɪ ə ɪ 不穩定(上)

July 29. Because the internship at your bank begins on Wednesday,
因為你們的實習周三7/27開始,我會缺序前面3天

July 27, I would need to miss the first three days. Would it be possible
有可能我在7/27之後的下周一再開始嗎?

for me to start on the following Monday instead? I believe this course
我知道這個珠程會幫助我股票分析師的實習 所以我希望你

will assist me in my work as a stock analyst intern, so I hope that you

will still allow me to take advantage of the internship opportunity.
能讓我利用(得到)這個實習機會。

I look forward to your reply.

Sincerely,          * volatile          → The situation in that area was tense,
Kenny Gould      易變的,易揮發的      dangerous and volatile.
                 Gasoline is volatile.   狀況危險,一觸即發

以實習活動長官的身分回信,提出一個解決方法

Directions: Reply to Mr. Gould as Louise Minter, the director of the
internship program. Offer ONE solution to Mr. Gould's
ɔ u ə
problem.
n. 解答,解決辦法

92

# Questions 6-7: Respond to a written request

## 答題範例

**Question 7**

＊relevant
adj. 有關的，有意義的

→I found much of my course
was not really relevant.
我發視我所學的課程
沒有太意思

Hi, Kenny,

你的課程聽起來很有趣

Thank you for your e-mail. Your course sounds interesting, and it is
而且絕對和我們的行業相關    你會想知道這件事的,
certainly relevant to our industry. You will want to know that,
因為今年有好多實習申請者.
because there were so many applicants for the internship positions
我們決定提供兩個整服實習課程，而不是一個
this year, we decided to offer two month-long internship sessions
7/27是第一期，第二期8/3開始，8/28結束
instead of one. The July 27 session will be first; the second will
這應該可以減輕(去除)
begin on August 3 and wrap up on August 28. This should alleviate
任何的行程衝突.
any scheduling conflict.
v. 減輕, 緩和
關於全職有新職位，我們會在二期實習都結束之後    alleviate
Regarding full-time paid positions, we'll decide which interns to hire    to light | v
決定哪位實習生我們要以永遠的基礎雇用
on a permanent basis only after both sessions are over. We will    alleviation
我們會在9月之前做出那些決定.
make those decisions by September. These positions have a start    levity
date of September 15. 這些職位9/15開始上班    n. 輕率. 不穩定. 多變
This is no occasion for
Please call me so we can finalize your plans.    levity.
這不是鬧著玩的
Regards,    ＊permanent    ←→ impermanent
Louise Minter    lasting    momentary
constant    temporary
stable    transient 一時的, 瞬間的
steady
enduring    → Her feelings of depression
durable    was transient.
他低潮的心情一下就沒有了

GO ON TO THE NEXT PAGE.

# Questions 8: Write an opinion essay

## Question 8

**Directions:** Read the question below. You have 30 minutes to plan, write, and revise your essay. Typically, an effective response will contain a minimum of 300 words.

下面的論述你同意還是不同意?
Do you agree or disagree with the following statement?

Schools should require that students learn how to play a musical instrument. Do you agree? Use specific reasons and examples to explain your answer.

學校應該要求學生學習如何彈奏樂器
你同意嗎?
提供特定的例子(明確的)例子和理由來解釋你的答案

例文結構:                        〈開頭:主題句點出
1 從各科目下手.有好有壞  — 起        不贊同
2 音樂優點              — 承
3 可是強迫學習是不好的 — 轉
4 不應該強迫           — 結論(合)

# Questions 8: Write an opinion essay

*compulsory
drive
adj. 必須做的. 強迫的

*algebra n. 代數

*calculus n. 算數

*resent v. 憤慨
resentful adj. 含怒的

答題範例

## Question 8

針對這個問題的簡短回應是：不. 學生不應該被要求學習樂器

My short answer to the question is: No, students should not be required to learn a musical instrument.

我的成長過程中, 音樂不是強迫性的 (上), 但是我一年級時參加學校樂隊, 最後學到

When I was growing up, music was not compulsory; however, I joined the school band in first grade, and eventually learned to play the piano, drums, and guitar. Music came easily because I loved to play more than anything else. On the other hand, I hated chess, history, and anything related to math. Of course, I was forced to study math along with chemistry and all the other subjects I didn't care about. To be honest, I still hate math, I never use it, and I've got no business in a scientific laboratory. If anything, forcing me to learn algebra and calculus just made me resentful. It's one thing to expose kids to things like music, art, dance, and theater; it's quite another to force it upon them. I don't think it works in the long run as a positive influence.

在一個鍋的教育系統中. 學生曝在一個很多科目. 教候, 尤其是藝術的高項程.

In a well-rounded system, students are exposed to a wide range of subjects and disciplines, especially the arts. Research has suggested that learning a musical instrument is beneficial to a child's brain development. It's said that music makes you smarter, happier, and more productive. Although listening to music is good, actively playing musical instruments is even more useful for learning cognitive skills. →有認知的知識 →知覺. 記憶. 思維都算

gnos = know

There is no denying the benefits of playing a musical instrument. Yet, it can't be forced on someone with any more success than forcing mathematics on me was. Most music enthusiasts see playing an instrument as a stress reliever, but for students who are not musically inclined it's just another thing to worry about. What's more, providing compulsory music lessons to students who have no interest in them—or any kind of arts for that matter—would not help them at all. I shake my head when I think of how much money my parents wasted on a math tutor for me. I was never going to get it.

當我想到我父母花了許多錢在我的數學家教上時我就搖頭 無是絕對學不會的 預. 他們不會有動力.

Students should choose to learn something they care about. Otherwise, they won't be motivated and will eventually lose interest. This kind of learning brings a lot of negativity into a kid's life. Besides, if the music program was not subsidized by the government (read: tax dollars), it would create an unnecessary burden. Buying a musical instrument costs a lot of money and students from low-income families would not be able to afford it. Their parents might have to borrow money, which leads to greater stress on the family.

目前狀態無需改變. 學可以在無壓力, 或是事稍的情況下. 嘗試很多樂器

The current situation doesn't need to be changed. Students can try several instruments without feeling the pressure to master one. Hence, I believe it would be unwise to make it compulsory for students to learn a musical instrument.

因此, 我相信强迫學生學樂器是不明智的